PRAISE FOR THE MADISON NIGHT MYSTERY SERIES

"A terrific mystery is always in fashion—and this one is sleek, chic and constantly surprising. Vallere's smart styling and wry humor combine for a fresh and original page-turner—it'll have you eagerly awaiting her next appealing adventure. I'm a fan!"

— Hank Phillippi Ryan,
Agatha, Anthony, Macavity and Mary Higgins Clark Award-Winning Author of *The Other Woman*

"All of us who fell in love with Madison Night in *Pillow Stalk* will be rooting for her when the past comes back to haunt her in *That Touch of Ink*. The suspense is intense, the plot is hot and the style is to die for. A thoroughly entertaining entry in this enjoyable series."

— Catriona McPherson,
Agatha Award-Winning Author of the Dandy Gilver Mystery Series

"A fast-paced mystery with fab fashions, an appealing heroine, and a clever twist, *That Touch of Ink* is especially for fans of all things mid-century modern."

— *ReadertoReader.com*

"Vallere has crafted an extremely unique mystery series with an intelligent heroine whose appeal will never go out of style."

– *Kings River Life Magazine*

"Diane Vallere…has a wonderful touch, bringing in the design elements and influences of the '50s and '60s era many of us hold dear while keeping a strong focus on what it means in modern times to be a woman in business for herself, starting over."

— *Fresh Fiction*

"A humorous yet adventurous read of mystery, very much worth considering."

— Paul Vogel, *Midwest Book Review*

"Make room for Vallere's tremendously fun homage. Imbuing her story with plenty of mid-century modern decorating and fashion tips…Her disarmingly honest lead and two hunky sidekicks will appeal to all fashionistas and antiques types and have romance crossover appeal."

— *Library Journal*

"A multifaceted story...plenty of surprises...And what an ending!"

— Mary Marks,
New York Journal of Books

"If you are looking for an unconventional mystery with a snarky, no-nonsense main character, this is it...Instead of clashing, humor and danger meld perfectly, and there's a cliffhanger that will make your jaw drop."

— Abigail Ortlieb,
RT Book Reviews

"A charming modern tribute to Doris Day movies and the retro era of the '50s, including murders, escalating danger, romance...and a puppy!"

— Linda O. Johnston,
Author of the Pet Rescue Mysteries

"I love mysteries where I can't figure out who the real killer is until the end, and this was one of those. The novel was well written, moved at a smooth pace, and Madison's character was a riot."

— *ChickLit Plus*

"Strong mysteries, an excellent cast, chills, thrills and

laughter, and an adorable dog... if you haven't read a Madison Night mystery, what are you waiting for?"

— *Kittling Books*

"The writing was crisp with a solid plot that kept me engaged with Madison, Tex and the other supporting cast."

— *Dru's Book Musing*

"The strength of this series that Madison has changed, adapted, and grown over the course of the six books."

— *3 no 7 Looks at Books*

"...a well plotted mystery filled with great characters that will keep you hooked until you get to the final page."

— *Carstairs Considers*

"If you are looking for a suspenseful "whodunit" without the gore or horror of other genres, this book is definitely for you."

— BookTrib

THE GLASS BOTTOM HOAX

A Madison Night Mystery

THE GLASS BOTTOM HOAX

A Madison Night Mystery #12

A Polyester Press Mystery

www.polyesterpress.com

All rights reserved. No part of this book may be used or reproduced by any means, graphic, electronic, or mechanical, including photocopying, recording, taping or by any information storage retrieval system without the written permission of the publisher except in the case of brief quotations embodied in critical articles and reviews.

This is a work of fiction. Characters, places, and events are the product of the author's imagination or are used fictitiously. Any resemblance to real people, companies, institutions, organizations, or incidents is entirely coincidental. No affiliation with Doris Day or Metro-Goldwyn Mayer Studio is claimed or implied.

Copyright © 2024 by Diane Vallere

Cover design by Waxing Crescent Moon Covers

eBook ISBN: 9781954579743

Paperback ISBN: 9781954579750

Hardcover ISBN: 9781954579767

THE GLASS BOTTOM HOAX

A Madison Night Mystery

Diane Vallere

Polyester Press

To Cathy Cole

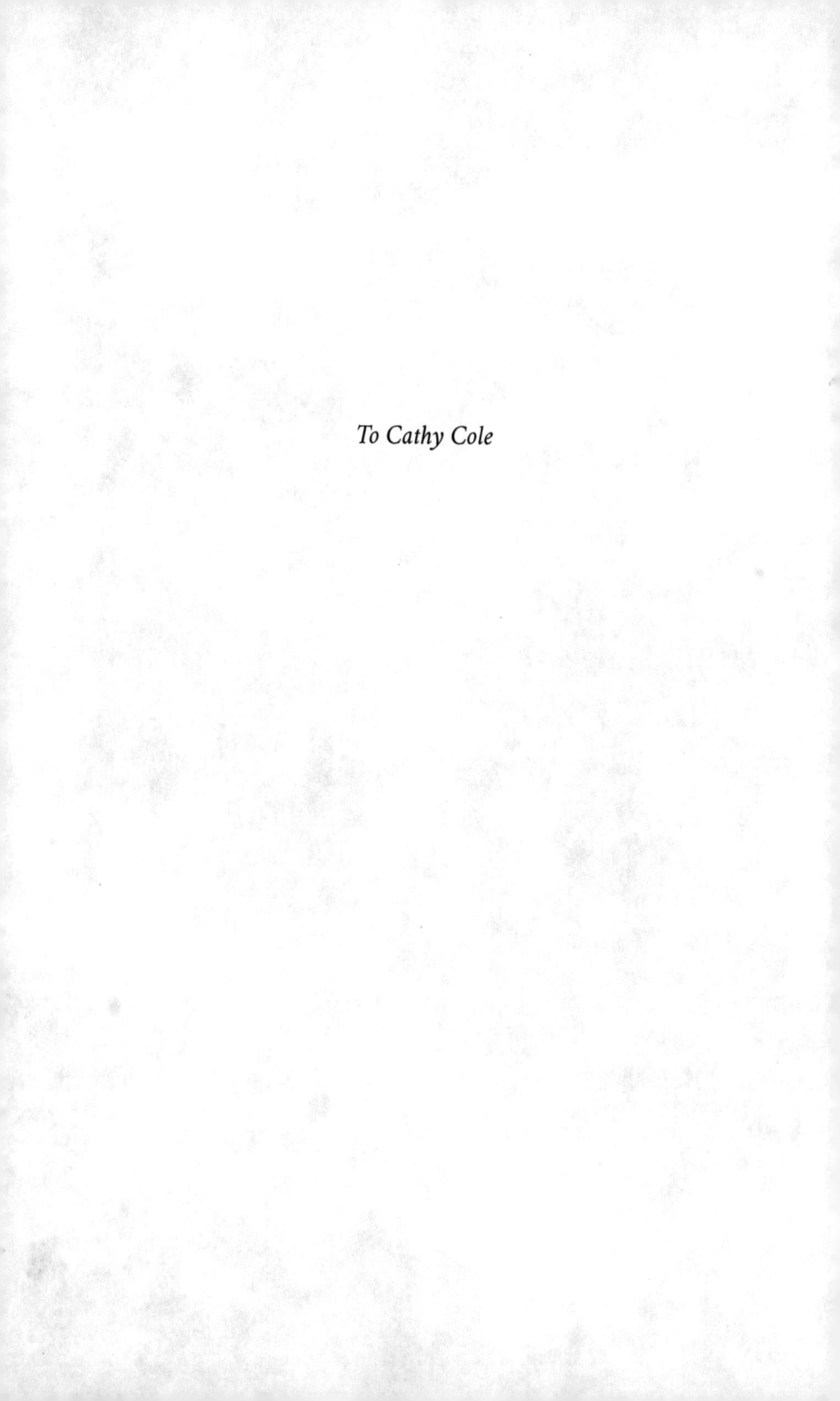

CHAPTER ONE

In terms of interview skills, I was rusty. A happily self-employed decorator, I had enough client appointments on my calendar to give me financial security. Finding myself across the desk from my potential new boss while a waiting room full of competition sat just outside her doors was a little unnerving. The only thing that helped was that I wasn't alone.

"I need a married couple," Nasty said.

Nasty was Donna Nast, former cop and current owner of Big Bro Security. She was also the sexy, barely thirty bombshell other side of the desk. She split her attention between me and my companion, Police Captain Tex Allen, while she waited for a response.

"We're not—" I glanced at Tex to gauge his reaction to what she'd said.

Tex leaned back in his chair, seeming totally at ease with the implication, incorrect as it was. He glanced at me and shrugged. "Hear her out."

Nasty held up her hand to quiet me. "Texas Luxury

Cruises approached me about managing security on their summer getaway fleet. They killed a story about a burglary ring on a recent cruise after their insurance company paid out hefty reimbursements, but they're afraid it might happen again. This is a big account, and it has the potential to be an ongoing gig. There's a hefty reward from the insurer if the stolen loot is recovered, but I've heard rumors about the owners, and I'm not sure if it's worth signing them on as a client."

"What rumors?" I glanced at Tex again. For someone who made his living interrogating people, he was noticeably quiet. Instead of looking at me, he kept his eyes trained on Nasty.

"Nothing I'm willing to believe without checking it out myself. That's why I need you."

"That's not what you said," I pointed out. I glanced over my shoulder at the door that separated the three of us from a lobby full of couples vying for a job, and things started to fall into place. "You don't need a married couple. You need a couple you can trust. You need two people who you can send on a cruise as paying customers who are willing to snoop around and report back to you if they find anything to legitimately keep you from taking this job."

"He's a cop. And you're—"

"Watch what you say next," I cautioned.

"—an unlikely spy." She leaned forward and rested her forearms on her desk. There was something urgent about her body language, and I sensed more than a potential whale client at the root of her concerns. "Nothing personal, Madison, but when people look at you, the first thing they think isn't 'This looks like a woman who might steal our secrets.'"

Blond and blue-eyed, I bore a striking resemblance to actress Doris Day and dressed accordingly to play up the likeness. In short, Nasty wasn't wrong.

"I can't go in there as a cop," Tex pointed out. "People treat cops differently. If someone on the cruise is hiding something, they're going to go into lockdown around me. You'll have more luck with an undercover as a deckhand."

Before the conversation could continue, a knock sounded on Nasty's door. "Hey, boss, it's Bruce," a deep male voice said.

"Give me a sec," Nasty told us. "Come on in," she called to the voice.

The door opened, and a beefy man in a faded gray T-shirt stood there. Describing him as white was a stretch considering most of his visible skin was covered with red, green, and blue tattoos. His head was shaved, but he had a ginger beard. The lone reassuring thing about him was that he'd called Nasty "boss."

"You wanted to see me?" he asked.

"Yes. It's about that job we discussed earlier." Nasty went to her desk and opened a drawer.

Bruce stood by the door. He didn't pay any attention to us, and I realized that to him, we were just one of many couples who had answered Nasty's ad. I didn't know why, but that fact tickled me.

Nasty handed over a folder. "There's some background information in there that you might find interesting."

"I'll look it over tonight. You want it back?"

"No, but best to shred it."

"You got it."

Something about watching Nasty interact with her team of security bros never ceased to impress me. She was efficient and confident. There was none of the tension one might expect in an environment with an attractive female boss and a team of testosterone-riddled employees. She'd told me once it was the opposite of what she'd experienced when she worked for the Lakewood Police Department as a patrol cop in uniform.

Bruce left, and Nasty spoke as if we hadn't been interrupted. "I don't want you as a cop," she told Tex, picking up right where we'd left off. "I want you as a person who happened to win a couple of complimentary cruise tickets from a raffle at a recent Big Bro new-client party. No badge, no backup. You'll be in the middle of the ocean with no jurisdiction over anybody on board."

"You don't think he can pull it off," I said, more than a little amused. "That's why you need me too." I faced Tex and gave him the full wattage of my smile. "Nasty thinks I bring out your softer side."

"She's not wrong," Nasty told Tex.

Tex's expression clouded. "There's a problem with your plan. Winners of a contest by definition don't belong where they're at. People pay attention to them. Everybody knows how they got there. If you're looking for a couple to go undercover, that's not the way to go about it."

Nasty and I looked at each other, and I suspected we were thinking the same thing. Neither one of us said it.

Tex folded his hands together and put them behind his head. He leaned back and propped his feet on the edge of Nasty's desk. "You don't have to tell me I'm right. That's the thing about being right most of the time. I don't have to hear it to know it's true."

It was a marvel of the human condition that Tex and I had found ourselves in a relationship. He was the last person

I would have expected to count on as my plus one. From the first moment we'd met, at a crime scene, he came on strong. Funnily enough, it was Nasty's bed he'd vacated that morning, which made our presence in her office that day all the more surreal.

It paid to be an adult. You learned to navigate all sorts of sticky situations.

A few seconds passed, and it seemed neither Nasty nor I was going to take Tex's bait. But the fact remained that he had a point. The minute we stepped foot on that cruise ship as the winners of Nasty's client contest, we would be at the mercy of the crew. If someone wanted to keep us from any nefarious business, we could easily be pushed away from the action like a puck on a shuffleboard court.

"We can say we bought a discount last-minute package," Tex said. "It gets us on the boat."

Nasty shook her head. "TLC doesn't do discounted packages. They're pushing the luxury part of 'Texas Luxury Cruises,' and that means protecting their pricing structure."

"What if I'm hired to do renovations on the boat?" I asked. "I'll be able to snoop around—"

Nasty held up her hand. "Texas Luxury Cruises is in the middle of a complete design overhaul of their fleet of ships. I can't bring an outside decorator on board. It's possible that TLC is part of the problem, so I'm limited in who I can get onto the ship. Aside from passengers and entertainment, everybody else is part of the crew."

"So we're going on as passengers." I glanced at Tex and laughed. "It's not like we can sing or dance."

I looked at Nasty. She stared at me—not Tex but me, just me—with an intensity that made me feel like a single-celled organism under a microscope. I narrowed my eyes and looked at Tex again.

He pulled his feet down from the desk and propped his elbow on it. He stared at me too.

"Why are you both looking at me like that?"

"It could work," Tex said.

"It could," Nasty agreed.

"What?" I asked again, putting a little more *oomph* into the question.

"You can pose as the entertainment. The crew will ignore you because it's their job to dote on the paying customers. You'll get behind-the-scenes access because technically, you work there. I'll arrange it through the entertainment director, so you'll have a contact. Nobody else will have to know your true identity."

"Not that I want to burst this little bubble of yours, but did you hear me say I can't sing or dance? I can't even convince Tex to go line dancing, and he probably learned how when he was five."

Tex leaned forward. "You have never once asked me to go line dancing."

"That's beside the point." I looked at him then at Nasty. "What I'm saying is that I don't think you want to burden us with the additional responsibility of getting people to believe we're the entertainment. One look at us and people will know we're not what we seem."

"You are."

"I am… what?"

"You're what you seem. You look like Doris Day. You dress like Doris Day. You are intimately familiar with the body of work of Doris Day."

"So?" I asked, proving Nasty's earlier point about my not

being smart enough to mastermind a covert intelligence operation. Then the proverbial light bulb went on. "Oh. No. That is not happening."

"It's pretty perfect," Nasty said. "I'll get you hired as a Doris Day impersonator on the cruise."

"But people don't care about Doris Day anymore. I mean, it's a travesty, but it's the truth. People want Barbie and Ken and Taylor Swift and Magic Mike."

"Not on a cruise ship. People expect a little cheese. Your shtick is exactly what we need."

"It's not shtick. It's who I am."

"That's what I'm counting on."

I pointed at Tex. "What about him? The only thing he's qualified to do is sexually harass the talent."

Tex grinned. It figured he would interpret my insult as a compliment.

"No," Nasty said. "Madison will get behind-the-scenes access, but if both of you are poking around the same places, it'll look suspicious. You need to be a regular guy along for the cruise."

"I thought we agreed the prize-winner deal wouldn't work," Tex said. His demeanor changed as his cover story folded.

"We'll go back to square one. I told you I needed a married couple. Madison will be the talent, and you'll be her manager spouse."

Tex looked at me. "What do you say, Night? Should we take married life for a test drive?"

CHAPTER TWO

I had to give Nasty credit. Once she settled on a plan, she executed it with remarkable efficiency. I'd long ago gotten over my first impression of her and learned she was smart, capable, and driven. That combination had helped me out of more than one tight spot. Somewhere along the way, we'd become unlikely friends.

Nasty owned Big Bro Security, one of the fastest-growing privately owned companies in Dallas, Texas. Nasty had started it herself after leaving the police force and grew it into a powerhouse. Taking on a client the size of Texas Luxury Cruises would add a sparkling gem to her portfolio and expand her territories. It was a bold move, very much her style, but I couldn't shake the notion that there was more to her concern than what she'd told us.

Still, it was a free cruise, and I was desperate for a getaway. Never mind that I was expected to sing for my supper.

The *New Nautilus* was scheduled to depart from Galveston, Texas, in three hours. (The old *Nautilus* went down somewhere around Cape Canaveral.) It was classified as a small ship, which made me think twice about ever going on a cruise classified as big. The ship was over six hundred feet long and accommodated four hundred guests. It had four restaurants, a spa, a movie library and viewing room, and a mini putting range, all in addition to the promenade deck, the lido deck, the mezzanine, and a sublevel complete with glass-bottom walls for the viewing of rare and exotic fish. A trio of pools, side by side, each with its own unique temperature, were at the back of the boat next to a stage where the Tossed Pebbles, a Rolling Stones tribute band, were expected to perform. My gig was a little less visible, relegated to the Nautilus Shell on the middle level of the ship, with performances scheduled for nine and eleven.

It was two days after Nasty first "hired" us. Tex and I had arrived early, as instructed, so we could meet our contact, the entertainment director, and board the ship early to start establishing our fake identities. I'd spent those two days attempting to reset my body's internal clock, sleeping in and staying up late to better fit the cruise-activity agenda. My performances were scheduled at night, and the last thing I needed was to get tired in the middle of a set.

Rocky, my shih tzu companion, was restless, unused to spending extended amounts of time in his carrier. He wore his service companion vest, though I'd long ago learned it was his sweet expression that gained him access to most restricted areas.

The drive from Dallas to Galveston was over four hours, and Tex had convinced his volunteer office manager, Imogene, to be our chauffeur. She had first come to work for him to conduct research for her mystery novel in progress, but the longer she worked for the Lakewood PD, the more I questioned whether her book would ever be done. Imogene seemed to enjoy the aura of *working on* a book more than *finishing* a book. She'd recently joined a critique group and told Tex she wanted to hole up in a hotel room to work on revisions. He had the department foot the bill in exchange for a ride.

"I'm giving this guy five more minutes," Tex said.

"And then what? It's not like we can just walk onto the boat if he doesn't get here. We have to pass through a security checkpoint, show identification, hand over Rocky's paperwork, the works. You're not a cop here. You can't just flash your badge and gain entry."

"You think I need my badge to get preferential treatment?"

"I think you underestimate how many doors open for you because you're the captain of the local police department. This cruise might not be the smooth sailing you're used to."

Whatever Tex was about to say got lost behind a deep, resonant horn. I wasn't expecting the sound, and I jumped, knocking over one of my suitcases. Rocky moved around in his carrier. Tex's dog, Wojo, was at home with his sister and her boys. They'd volunteered to watch Rocky, too, but I'd spent enough time with those boys to know Rocky was safer with me on a boat in the middle of the ocean.

Also, people expected the talent to be a little demanding.

A Filipino man in a white uniform suit hustled toward us. "Are you the Templetons?"

"Yes," we said in chorus, perhaps a little too eager to respond to our cover.

"I'm Homer Manalo." He nodded at Tex then me.

Even though Nasty had established our cover with the entertainment director, we'd all agreed to keep our actual identities confidential. Between a lawsuit with my business a few years ago then an identity mix-up that led to my obituary being published, I'd been in and out of the news a lot lately. Tex had issues to contend with too—namely, that people clammed up around cops. Nasty told us her contact would know we were there on her behalf, but other than that, he didn't know who we really were.

Homer, fortunately, was exactly as Nasty had described him. Six foot tall with brown skin, thick eyebrows, and full red lips, the sum total of which probably made him popular among the passengers. His uniform had the *New Nautilus* logo on a patch on his sleeve, and two gold stripes circled the left wrist of his jacket.

"I'm Madison. This is—"

"Her husband." Tex held out his hand. "Call me Tex."

Homer ignored Tex's outstretched hand. "Right. I'm putting you in a guest room on the starboard side. It might seem a little cramped at first, but we got a rush of last-minute passengers, and the upgraded rooms all filled. It would look suspicious if I put you in one of them since you're technically here for free."

"Sure." I smiled. "Whatever you need, it'll be fine."

Rocky yipped.

"What was that?" Homer looked around as if confused.

"My dog." My sunny disposition faltered, and I wrapped my arm around Rocky's mesh carrier. "He's my service companion. I have all of his required papers."

A few years ago, I'd completed the certification process so that Rocky could accompany me anywhere I went. In addition to having a chronic knee injury that flared up at the least convenient times, I'd been through enough emotionally challenging situations to make my argument persuasive. I held Rocky's carrier snug against my hip.

"Nobody told me there was a dog," Homer said.

"He's very well-behaved. I don't plan to take him out of the room except maybe in the downtime when none of your passengers are going to be up."

"Is this your first cruise?" he asked, not waiting for my response. "Even when pets are allowed on a cruise ship, they're quarantined in the kennel quarters on the bottom level of the boat. You can visit him, but he can't come to your room."

I turned my body away from Homer as if I could keep Rocky from hearing the words "kennel" and "quarantine."

Homer seemed to sense my reluctance. His voice softened, and he added, "The decks are open around the clock. We've got mambo lessons at midnight and yoga at dawn. The bartenders keep people plied with liquor. It would be dangerous for your dog to be among the passengers."

"I'll take responsibility for him." Tex took Rocky's carrier from my shoulder and hung it over his. His actions and his voice were strong and commanding. He could turn on his alpha male personality when necessary, though usually, "necessary" involved a dead body, an open homicide, and a person of interest. Good thing we were only there to investigate the crew.

I didn't know whether Homer was going to let Tex get away with breaking a rule so early in our trip, but on the off chance that I could distract the purser, I asked a question that had nothing to do with my dog.

"How do you know Donna Nast?"

"Who?"

"The owner of Big Bro Security. She arranged for us to be on this cruise, remember? She worked with you to establish our cover stories so we could poke around the ship and find out what's going on here. You're the only person on the cruise to know why we're here, so I figured you must know her pretty well for her to trust you."

"I wouldn't call it trust." Homer glanced to his left and his right, even though the ship's security hadn't started allowing people on board. I waited for him to elaborate on his comment after he confirmed we were alone, but he left his statement dangling in the breeze like a worm at the end of a fishhook. I turned my head slightly to see if Tex had noticed. He stared at Homer with his unflinching cop gaze. Tex was clearly waiting for Homer to say or do something too.

Homer reached into his pants pocket and pulled out two flat key cards. "You're in room two-oh-one. I can't take you there myself, but if you follow the carpet to the end of the aisle, you'll find a staircase that will take you up to the lido deck, and around the corner from the poolside bar is another staircase that will get you to the second floor. Once you're there, go to the end of the starboard side. Your room is the second to the last."

The directions were complicated, and anybody else would have attempted to repeat them to ensure they remembered them correctly, but only one word of them stood out to me.

"Stairs?" I asked.

"The help is expected to take the stairs so the elevators remain free for the paying guests. I might be able to get an exception made for you, Mrs. Templeton, since the passengers might like mingling with the talent, but not your husband." He looked at Tex, who somehow had managed not to react to any number of questionable statements.

"Understood," Tex said. Rocky yipped from his carrier, and Tex pulled a dog biscuit out of his pocket, unzipped the corner of the carrier, and dropped the treat in.

"What did you just put in his carrier?" Homer asked.

"Dog biscuit."

"You can't bring food on board the cruise."

"It's a *dog biscuit.*"

Homer held his palm out. Tex scowled.

Homer said, "Mr. Templeton, if you want to go undetected on this cruise, you'd best follow the rules that everybody else follows. If you don't, people are going to ask questions. It's bad enough I have to babysit your wife. I'm not prepared to babysit you too."

Tex widened the opening on Rocky's carrier and reached in. He and Rocky engaged in a brief tug-of-war while Tex did what he could to get the biscuit back. Rocky wasn't used to Tex taking away treats, and he growled. Shih tzus weren't the most menacing of dogs, so the effect was cuter than if he were a Rottweiler.

"That's it," Homer said. "We can't risk the safety of the passengers with a hostile dog on board. You're going to have to get him off the boat."

"Exactly what are you proposing?" I asked. "We're in Galveston. We live in Dallas. I can't call a friend for a handoff."

Homer had a radio clipped to his belt, and a blast of static sounded. "Passengers coming on board. All crew needed for welcome."

"I have to go," Homer said. He pointed at the carrier. "Give that rat to someone in customs. They'll keep it in short-term storage while we're gone. You can pick it up when we get back."

CHAPTER THREE

I WAITED UNTIL HOMER WAS OUT OF SIGHT BEFORE TURNING to Tex. "Did you hear that? There is no way Rocky is being handed off to a random employee in customs so he can sit in a storage bin in Galveston. Call Nasty. Tell her we're out."

"Not so fast." Tex stared down the hallway in the direction Homer had gone. "That guy's hiding something. I don't know what, but we're here to find out."

"I don't care," I said. "I'm not using Rocky as bait, and I'm not leaving him with a stranger."

"Nobody said you were." Tex held Rocky's carrier out to me, and I took it. He pulled out his phone and made a call. "Are you still in the area? Come on back. I need you to watch Madison's dog while we're gone. She'll meet you in the parking lot." He was silent for a moment. "Done." He hung up.

"Who did you just call?" I asked.

"Imogene."

"I thought she was going to tune out the world to work on revisions."

"If Imogene writes five words on that book, it'll be a miracle. Last time I asked, she said she wanted to add some pirates."

"I thought her mystery was set in modern-day Dallas."

"Exactly."

Rocky turned around inside his carrier, causing it to tilt. Tex shrugged out of his suit jacket, an unlikely wardrobe choice that fit his cruise character. Underneath it, he wore a white golf shirt. He draped the jacket over the carrier then took the carrier again. "Head back the way we came in. Find people. Any people. Tell them who you are and ask how to get to our room."

"What are you going to do?"

"I'll take care of Rock."

I unzipped the side of the carrier and pulled Rocky out, nuzzling my face into his fur for a brief goodbye.

Rocky whimpered. His carrier smelled less than fresh. I unzipped the top wider and saw a small accident in the corner. He looked up at me. People who said animals didn't know how to communicate had never looked into the big round eyes of a troublesome shih tzu, because I knew in that moment that Rocky knew he'd done something wrong.

People who claimed it was easy to discipline a shih tzu were equally full of smoke, because one look into the big round eyes of an apologetic shih tzu was all it took to melt a heart, regardless of how troublesome said shih tzu might be.

I stroked Rocky's fur and reassured him that everything was okay. I pulled his leash out of my pocket and clipped it on, then I set him onto the pavement and used a plastic baggie over my hand to remove the offending turd from his carrier. I flipped the bag inside out and tossed it in a nearby trash bin.

Next, I handed Rocky's leash to Tex, who scooped him up. Rocky put his fluffy paws on Tex's shoulder and licked the side of Tex's face. To Tex's credit, he didn't act like that was a bad thing.

"I'll go find Imogene and meet you in our room," Tex said.

"You remember how to get there?"

"Homer's directions were the most complicated series of twists and turns he could have given us. That's a good thing. Now I have an excuse to get turned around and open some doors that should otherwise be off-limits."

"Just promise me you won't miss the boat."

"And miss seeing you perform? Not a chance."

There was a reason Tex and I made a good sleuthing team for Nasty, and it wasn't just that she knew us. I'd heard instructions to hand Rocky off to a stranger and got angry. Tex had heard an unspoken motivation to upset our lives. I heard complicated directions and got confused. Tex heard them and recognized an excuse to go where he wasn't supposed to be. As long as one of us paid attention to our surroundings and the other kept our story intact, we could do this. It was a simple enough cover—husband and wife, singer and along-for-the-free-shrimp-cocktail husband. Nothing suspicious about that. Nasty probably recognized our unique ability to be both offended and effective.

A skinny man in a white uniform rounded the corner, causing a near collision with Tex and Rocky. "What are you doing here?" he asked.

"We're the Templetons," I said.

"I don't care who you are. You can't be here."

"Homer met us for early entry," Tex said. "My wife is your headlining act."

I watched him. The word "wife" slid off his tongue more

easily than I would have expected from a lifelong bachelor. But Tex had adopted undercover roles before, more than once, and I knew our assignment would be more challenging for me than for him.

"Homer needs to stop making decisions without consulting the captain."

"Are you the captain?" I asked.

"I'm the boatswain. Lenny Robinson. It's my job to make sure the boat is in shipshape shape."

I grinned, assuming that was intended to be funny. Lenny scowled at me. He shifted his attention to Rocky. "Is that a dog?"

"We're just saying goodbye."

Tex left me standing on the dock with Lenny and went in search of Imogene.

Lenny seemed to notice our luggage scattered around my feet. "Did Homer leave you here with your luggage too?"

"Yes."

Lenny considered that for a moment then reached up and readjusted his hat. His expression changed from annoyed to frustrated. It was a subtle shift, but it made him seem a little less antagonistic.

"Sorry about my attitude. It's been one thing after another this morning. I'll escort you to your room and have your luggage delivered by a porter. You said you're the talent? That puts you on the top deck. Let me see your key card."

I held out my card, and Lenny scanned it with a handheld device. His face clouded as he read the display. "There's been a mix-up. Someone put you on the second floor, past the lido deck. That's where the janitorial crew sleeps."

"Homer said there was a last-minute rush of passengers, and it was this or nothing."

"Not true. This cruise is only partially booked. Nostalgia cruises from the sixties are on their way out. People want eighties. Hair bands and pop stars." He looked me up and down. "No offense."

"None taken."

Lenny handed me my key card. "I can't do anything about your room, but the captain can. In the meantime, let's get your belongings out of the hallway. I'll get a luggage cart." He went in a different direction from Homer.

Already, I'd noticed that a cruise ship offered any number of hallways through which to disappear, and until I understood the layout, I wouldn't know who went where and why.

Being the talent on a cruise ship meant looking the part. For most people, that would be a challenge, but it wasn't for me. I regularly dressed in vintage from the fifties and sixties. My business model relied on buying out estates, and the women who decorated with Norcrest mermaids and Witco wall art often had closets bursting with double knit polyester ensembles.

Today I wore a yellow shirtwaist dress from the estate of Sydney Cavero-Egusquiza. Sydney was the kind of woman who defined herself by her award-winning apple pie. She'd had a closet filled with cotton dresses in every color of the rainbow, along with a vast assortment of coordinating aprons. Among other items I found in her estate was a film reel that showed her being interviewed for a local TV show after receiving a blue ribbon at the Texas State Fair. The best thing about her wardrobe? No stains.

I owned more clothes than I could wear in five

lifetimes, but in addition to the garments I incorporated into my wardrobe, the cruise offered an opportunity to also wear the cocktail dresses that hung in plastic garment bags in my spare bedroom closet. I planned to sing along to Doris Day recordings that would mask any sour notes that escaped from me while performing. Nasty had had to pay some clearance fees to make it all legit, but it was this or hire musicians, and it would have been darn near impossible to keep my cover around people who performed for a living.

I picked up my vintage turquoise Samsonite train case and walked down the hallway. Voices carried to me. I rounded a corner, and a long line of people waited outside of a black velvet rope. On the other side of the rope stood a row of cruise ship employees. Most wore white uniforms with a blue-and-yellow patch on the sleeve. A woman with a toothy smile stood at the front of the group. After each person had his or her identification checked by a security team, the woman greeted them and waved them past the velvet rope. An anticipatory energy filled the air. People were eager to get on board and start their vacations.

Not for the first time since agreeing to work the cruise on behalf of Nasty, I thought about what she'd asked us to do. Someone on this boat was not who they seemed, and Nasty needed us to ferret out who that was. But every person who worked on the *New Nautilus* had been security screened. They'd passed deep background checks, not just the cursory ones most employers conducted. Someone had been able to get a position on the ship after jumping through enough hoops to appear to be on the up-and-up and then, after securing employment, set about conducting crimes. It was as if the criminal plan came after the job, as if the culprit had never considered becoming a thief until after he or she discovered how easy it would be.

Temptation was a powerful thing.

As I stood in the hallway and watched people pass through the security checkpoint, I marveled at the size of the crowd boarding the ship. The passengers included male-female couples, male-male couples, and female-female couples. There was no clear demographic for the guests aside from them being over forty, as the marketing copy had described. Two Black women in their late sixties spotted me and pointed. They grinned and waved. I turned around and looked behind me. The hallway was empty. I turned back, and the women giggled.

I didn't realize I'd been joined by Homer.

"They're excited to see you perform," he said. His attitude had softened from our first encounter, and I chalked it up to first-day stresses and the extra complication of him having to babysit me and Tex.

"They're supposed to be excited about unlimited buffets and shuffleboard."

"This is a nostalgia cruise," Homer said. "The entire theme is built around 1966. This ship has been out of rotation while the owners had it reimagined for the theme. The decorator is around here somewhere."

"The decorator gets a gratis cruise?" I'd never once considered bidding on cruise ship jobs, but that sounded like a good perk.

"She didn't finish the job on time. If you ask me, they should have fired her and gotten somebody else to wrap things up. Maybe a decorator from Dallas who specializes in mid-century modern design?"

I'd been watching the line of people getting onto the ship,

but Homer's very specific comment could be taken only one way. Nasty had reassured me that nobody, not even Homer, would know who Tex and I *really* were, only that we'd been hired to work for her. Slowly, I turned and searched his face.

"I wouldn't worry so much about how I know Donna Nast if I were you. I know why you're here, Ms. Night. I can make your stay easy, or I can make it hard. Think about that before you go poking around where you don't belong."

CHAPTER FOUR

I'd counted on Homer to be an ally. If he knew our real identities, then we were already at risk. And for a person who was supposed to be our man on the inside, he was acting a lot like he didn't want us there.

"What exactly do you think you know about me?" I asked.

"I'd worry more about what *you* think you know. And then I'd forget it." He squeezed my arm hard enough to leave a shadow of pain where his fingertips pressed into my flesh, then he left me alone and joined the rest of the crew.

If nothing else, Homer's behavior was suspicious enough to note. I wanted to race to the room and tell Tex, but Tex was doing his own investigating, and we would be more effective if we divided and conquered. I took a bolstering breath and marched to the crowd.

One of the Black women—dressed in a head-to-toe ensemble of pale-pink tank top, pale-pink capri pants, and gauzy white linen shirt, looked at her friend, who wore a version of the same outfit in aqua, and exclaimed, "You're Doris Day!"

"I'm Madison," I said. A few feet away, a *New Nautilus* photographer snapped a picture of us. If nothing else, our colorful clothing choices would make for a pleasing composition.

"Who's Madison?" the women asked in chorus. The one in aqua added, "Doris Day never played anybody named Madison."

The one in pink said, "There was a Jan, a Jennifer, a Judy, a Jane—" She ticked the names off on her fingers.

"Doris Day liked *J* names," the woman in aqua told me.

Pink continued. "Beverly, Kitty, Carol, Cathy—"

"There was a Margaret," Aqua Lady exclaimed as if she were a participant on a game show.

"*My* name is Madison," I said. "Madison Templeton."

"Templeton!" they exclaimed in chorus. "There was a Templeton, but it wasn't her. It was Rod Taylor in—"

I held up my hand. "Doris Day played Carol Templeton opposite Rock Hudson in *Lover Come Back*," I said. "You're thinking of *Bruce* Templeton from *The Glass Bottom Boat*."

"She's right," Aqua said. She turned to me. "I should have assumed you knew your Doris Day trivia."

"We're the Stork sisters," Pink said. "I'm Meg. She's Mavis."

The woman in aqua reached up and fingered a thin gold necklace that spelled out her name as if the introduction reminded her that she was wearing it. "You're our favorite actress," Mavis said.

Through my life, I'd encountered all sorts of people who shared my love of Doris Day (and more than one who vehemently didn't), so I never really knew how these conversations were going to go.

"I'm not—"

The women shared a look of concern. Meg turned to me. "Is this your first cruise?"

"How did you guess?"

"It's customary for the impersonators to take on the role of the person they're playing. You're not supposed to be a person singing Doris Day songs. You're supposed to be Doris Day."

"But Doris Day is—"

Mavis put her hands over her ears. "Don't say it!"

Meg put her hands on Mavis's hands and lowered them. "My sister can be melodramatic. But she's right. We can help you if you want. We'll be like groupies. It tends to help the talent stay in character when there's someone working the crowd."

"How do you know so much about how this works?"

Meg said, "We go on cruises all the time. We're so well-known around here we're practically part of the crew."

When Nasty had first briefed Tex and me about the job, it seemed cut-and-dried. Someone on the inside was stealing from the passengers, and Nasty's company had been hired by the insurance company to expose the guilty party. She said there was a considerable reward for recovery of the stolen items and/or capture of the burglars, along with a hefty contract for Big Bro Security should they come through with a satisfying resolution. Those two facts should have made the investigation a slam dunk for her, so the fact that it wasn't meant there was a bigger red flag than what she'd told us.

Inside a folder in my room was a list of every employee assigned to the voyage from Galveston to Cozumel, and I intended to seek as many of them as possible to catch the burglar. It had never occurred to me that there might be cruise regulars, so I suddenly realized the massive flaw in my calculations. A member of the crew would know the layout of the ship and the activities schedule, which might make it easy to know when rooms would be vacant, but a passenger would be able to play dumb, get lost, and find themselves in places they had no business being.

Tex was counting on that right now.

The crew would likely be held to other standards, like employees of a retail store who were expected to carry clear handbags. A passenger, though? Nobody would search their luggage. Nobody would accuse them of theft. The opposite was probably true. If the cruise line wanted their regulars to return again and again, they might even hand them a few extras on their way out.

Meg and Mavis Stork looked unlikely to be criminal masterminds, but maybe that was by design.

"Ladies, it was a pleasure meeting you. I hope to see you at dinner tonight."

The sisters shared another expression. Mavis put her hand on her aqua tummy and looked away.

Meg said, "Mavis gets a touch of seasickness the day we depart. You probably won't see us tonight. We usually have food in our room while we adjust to the rocking of the boat."

"Of course. Take care of yourself." I looked at the line ahead of me. The passengers moved slowly, but more people were on the boat and waiting to board. The chatter of enthusiastic passengers had risen, making it difficult to hear casual conversation.

While we stood together, my cell phone buzzed against my hip. I'd been warned that upon departure, cell service wouldn't be as reliable as it was on land, and internet service would be even worse. I checked the screen. It said "Captain

Allen." I swiped the screen to answer before anybody saw the display.

"Where are you?" Tex asked.

"I'm at the entrance point. People are boarding the ship, and I thought it would be a good idea to greet them." I looked up at the sisters to see if they were eavesdropping. Not only were they making no secret of the fact that they were listening in, but Meg also waggled her eyebrows at me.

"Listen carefully," Tex said. "Lenny talked to the captain about our room problems. He said to give us an upgrade to one of the vacant luxury suites. And Imogene was thrilled to dog-sit. She said you can FaceTime with Rock during the cruise if you want."

"I'm sure *Rock* would love that."

Tex preferred to call Rocky by his given name and not his expanded nickname, as if adding a *y* somehow lowered Tex's testosterone levels. Despite having named my dog after Doris Day's most famous co-star, I had added the perky *y* in Rocky's puppy years, mostly because the name fit his personality.

I glanced at Meg and Mavis again then turned my back to them. "Will this affect our arrangement?"

"Not sure yet. Normally, I'd be thrilled with the change in plans, but not with this job hanging over our heads. Homer's room assignment snafu would have put us in the action. Now we're on our own." He sighed. "A member of the crew is supposed to meet us by our original room to move our stuff. Do you remember how to get there?"

"I'll do my best."

After disconnecting, I turned around. Somewhere during my private conversation with Tex, the Storks had moved on to another cluster of people. The crowd had dissipated as new passengers made their way to their rooms. It seemed like a good idea to head off toward mine too.

I made my way through the disappointingly decorated hallways following signs that pointed to the lido deck. Somewhere along the way I must have taken a right when I should have gone left and found myself thoroughly confused.

While I paused to study a map of the ship, I heard a door close behind me. I crept down the hall. No other rooms were in that part of the ship, but there was an emergency exit at the end of the carpeted hall. I walked toward the exit and pushed the door open. It revealed a staircase up and a staircase down. There was no sign of a person having gone through there recently. I stood for a moment, straining my ears for a sound, but nothing came. Reluctantly, I stepped back and let go of the door. I didn't expect to run into a person, and I stifled a scream at the contact.

"Hey! Hi! Ho!" The woman held up her hands in surrender. "Are you Madison?"

"Yes. You startled me."

"I'm Willow, the first officer. Are you okay?"

Willow was dressed in the same uniform as the rest of the crew: white jacket with the *New Nautilus* logo embroidered above the breast pocket, white trousers, white deck shoes. Her hair was cut short and swept away from her face. She wore little makeup save for a tinted lip balm. My hometown of Dallas was filled with women who kept the beauty industry thriving with their salon visits, but life on a boat clearly had different demands.

"I'm fine, I think." I forced a note of humor into my shaky voice. "Just waiting for my husband to meet me with a member of the crew."

"About that. The purser's missing, so we're short-staffed

at check-in. I can't spare anybody to move you into your new room until tomorrow morning. I'm sorry about the inconvenience. This isn't supposed to happen."

I could feel waves of nervousness coming off the young first officer. She'd scared me when I backed into her, but I could tell my reaction scared her too. She was younger than the other crew members I'd met, likely more inexperienced too. I didn't need to complicate matters.

"It's fine," I reassured her. "But if you don't mind, I'd like to relax before dinner. If my original room is still empty, I'll use that. What's the shortest way there?"

"The crew is supposed to stick to the staircases and leave the elevators open for the paying customers." Willow looked annoyed by that detail. "But you're talent, so you get to go where the passengers go. It'll be faster for you to go back down the hall and up the stairs to the shuffleboard court. On the other side is a flight of stairs to the lower decks. Normally, you'd get hung up with guests, but everybody's checking into their rooms, so if you go now, you'll get there without incident."

I thanked her and left. I passed the door and kept going through the exit then up three steps to the shuffleboard court. That was where I stopped.

Willow had said I could make it to my room this way without incident, but she'd been mistaken. Because lying across the shuffleboard court with a knife jutting out of his chest was the body of Homer Manalo, the Filipino entertainment director, the only person on the ship who knew Tex's and my real reason for being on the boat.

CHAPTER FIVE

THE SECOND THING I SAW, AFTER THE BODY OF THE entertainment director lying across the shuffleboard court, was the gulf of Galveston getting smaller, drifting away from the boat. Except it wasn't the gulf drifting away from the boat but the boat moving away from the gulf. Somewhere between me chatting with the Stork sisters and me ending up on the lido deck, the ship had sailed out to sea.

There were protocols to follow when it came to finding a body. Sad to say, I was more than familiar with them. It was how I'd first met Tex, after he arrived at a crime scene to investigate a body under the wheels of my car outside the pool where I swam morning laps. The brain didn't always default to practical thoughts at such times, and I found myself wondering if Tex and I were destined to always be surrounded by death and water.

The longer I stood on the shuffleboard court and stared at Homer's body, the more questions cropped up. They were like bluebonnets blooming across a Texas on-ramp in springtime, filling my brain to the point of distraction. I didn't know the expected chain of command for reporting something like this on a cruise ship, but I did know there was one person on the boat I could trust—Tex.

I pulled my phone out and called him. The call failed. I changed the settings and logged onto the ship Wi-Fi and tried again, this time with success.

"Where are you?" he asked.

"Are you alone?"

"No."

"Then listen carefully and don't say a word. I'm on the shuffleboard court with Homer." I peeked at Homer's body. "Someone stabbed him. He's dead."

"Stay put. I'll be right there."

The beauty of being in a relationship with a high-ranking police officer was that he understood the need to act first and ask questions later. I wasn't thrilled about standing guard over a dead body, but my problems were far less severe than Homer's.

The hot sun beat down on me. As a rule, I coated myself from head to toe with the strongest sunscreen I could find, and today was no different. I didn't know what direct sunlight and one-hundred-plus degrees of heat would do to Homer's body, but I didn't think it would be good for evidence collection. While I waited for Tex to arrive, I pulled a blue plastic tarp from the shuffleboard equipment and loosely draped it over Homer's body. The plastic was rigid and pitched like a tent. I moved sacks of sand to the corners of the tarp to anchor them, then I sat on the deck and put my head in my hands to get a handle on my nausea.

Maybe the Stork sisters were smart to sit the first day out.

Tex did not arrive alone. I heard two male voices getting

closer and recognized one. Dull footsteps pounded up the carpeted stairs, and Tex burst onto the court with Lenny, the boatswain.

"Where is he?" Lenny turned in a circle and scanned the landing.

Tex didn't do his usual Tex thing. He came over to where I sat huddled against the wall. He stooped and put his arms around me then held me in a comforting embrace. He put his mouth next to my ear and said, "You're a Doris Day impersonator, and I'm your husband. I'm not a cop. I'm not in charge. It's not up to us how this gets handled. Neither one of us has any experience with a situation like this, but if we watch the way the crew handles the emergency, we might learn something. Now, more than ever, we have to maintain our cover." He pulled his head back and tipped my chin up so I was looking directly at him.

Tex was right. I put my hand on his forearm to keep him from walking away. I called out to Lenny, "He's under the tarp."

Lenny moved a sack of sand and lifted the corner of the tarp. He stared at Homer's body for a few seconds then pulled the corner of the tarp down and replaced the weight. He shielded his eyes and looked toward the coast, just as I had.

"I didn't sign on for this," he said, though it didn't seem like he intended to direct it at either Tex or me. He walked away from the body and leaned against the railing. Wind blew against his face, pushing his hair back.

I looked at Tex. "Is he going to jump?"

"Might make our job easier if he does. That's the kind of behavior that makes a person look guilty."

Lenny turned around and faced us. "I have no right to ask

this of you, but can you keep this quiet? My job puts me in charge of the crew." He pointed at the tarp. "Homer is crew. I'll notify the captain, but first, I've got to get Homer out of the public area before a guest sees him."

"We won't say anything," I said. "Will we, honey?"

"Mum's the word."

Tex stood and held out his hands to pull me up. I took full advantage of the offer. When I was on my feet, he put his arm around my waist and embraced me. Tex wasn't big on public displays of affection, so I assumed his gesture was part of his cover. I didn't mind, considering I was shaking.

Mr. and Mrs. Templeton had no reason to stay on the lido deck with the boatswain and the body. I glanced at Tex and tipped my head toward the stairs. He nodded. We turned to leave. I glanced over my shoulder and saw Lenny still rooted in place, staring at the blue plastic tarp. He seemed to have been immobilized by the situation.

"I think Lenny needs help," I whispered.

"If Lenny needs help, Lenny has to ask for help. Normal people don't volunteer to help move bodies."

"I resent the implication."

"I didn't know I made one."

"Excuse me, Mr. Templeton?" Lenny's voice, thin and reedy, called out. "Do you think—I mean—can you—I'm sorry to ask. Could you help me move Homer?"

Tex and I looked at each other. Unless Lenny had exceptional hearing or had planted listening devices on our persons when we weren't looking, there was no way he'd overheard us. We spun around. Lenny hadn't moved, but his face had lost some of its color.

"Won't the police want to see where his body was found?"

I asked. Tex's hand squeezed my waist and not in a way that felt romantic.

"Don't listen to her," Tex said quickly. "She's a fan of true-crime shows." He let go of me, and I stumbled backward. I put my hand out and moved toward the wall for stability. The cruise ship was remarkably steady but the situation had left me with vertigo.

Nasty had provided me with a dress code and a checklist of handy things to pack for the cruise. ("Take magnets," she'd said. "The ship is made of metal. Take Chapstick. You'll be surprised by how dry your skin gets.") She'd told me what to expect. ("Your rings will feel big. Your dreams will be vivid. Your bad knee will feel good.") She never once told me I'd feel like I was trying to stand on two rubber bands.

Lenny mistook my found-a-body vertigo for land legs. "You'll get used to being on the boat by tomorrow," he said. "Hold on to the railing. It'll help your legs stabilize."

I nodded. Tex left me and joined Lenny, and I went to the railing. I saw no point in turning around and watching them do whatever it was they were going to do. Tex would tell me if anything suspicious happened while my back was turned. Like him, I knew it was more important for me to act in a way that didn't look suspicious, and that meant taking the advice of the one person on the lido deck who had done the whole cruise thing before.

The one *living* person.

I wrapped my fingers around the railing and closed my eyes. The warmth of the sun felt good, as did the cool metal under my palms. A gentle breeze tossed my hair. I reached my left hand up and held my hair away from my face, but as soon as I let go, it blew back. Behind me came the sound of plastic crinkling, men grunting, shoes squeaking against the shuffleboard court. Seagulls overhead. "Satisfaction," played live by the Tossed Pebbles—a little heavy on the drums.

"Mrs. Templeton?" Lenny called out.

I looked back. Lenny and Tex stood about six feet apart. Between them, a large roll of blue plastic sat on the ground. I kept one hand on the railing. "Yes?"

"We're going to need someone to hold the door open for us."

Even Tex looked embarrassed by Lenny's request.

"Of course." I turned toward the ocean, staring out at the shoreline, wondering what, exactly, Nasty had signed us up for. I dropped my gaze from the land to the water and stared into the choppy greenish-blue sea.

That's when I saw the mermaid.

CHAPTER SIX

I leaned over the railing and stared into the brackish water. White peaks of foam dotted the surface, making it difficult to see below.

"Madison!" Tex cried. Seconds later, his arms were wrapped around me in a bear hug from behind.

I pointed at the ocean surface. "Did you see that?"

"See what?"

"The mermaid."

"Night—" Tex said. He caught his use of my last name a moment too late and tacked on "mare," which made no sense to anyone listening. "Your brain is playing tricks on you."

Lenny came over and stood on the other side of me. "No, she's right. That's our mermaid."

As troubled as Lenny had been at seeing Homer's body, he seemed completely comfortable with the idea of a mermaid swimming alongside the boat. Comfortable enough to claim her as their own. "See?" He pointed at a bright-orange mermaid tail undulating under the water. The tail flipped up into the air, splashing water, then disappeared. A couple of seconds later, a woman's head broke the surface. She had long red hair that fanned out around her shoulders, and she wore thick scuba goggles, which she moved to the top of her head, revealing her tanned face and broad smile.

"Ahoy there!" She waved with one hand while she sculled the water with the other.

"Ahoy!" Lenny waved back.

"That's Jennifer. She's the dive instructor. Once or twice a day, she puts on a mermaid costume and swims around the boat. Nobody knows what time she goes out, so it's always a surprise when someone spots her."

Jennifer wore an orange bikini top that matched her tail. She pulled her goggles into place and plunged below the surface. Her bright hair streamed behind her as she sliced through the dense blue green of the Galveston coastal waters, making it easy to see her. She swam around the side of the ship, where she disappeared from sight.

There was nothing like a mermaid sighting to distract someone from more urgent needs, but like most distractions, this one was temporary. Homer's bundled-up body was where Tex and Lenny had left it at the top of the staircase.

A female voice came over the ship's loudspeaker. "Welcome to the *New Nautilus*! After you settle into your guest quarters, join us for cocktails at sunset by the Horizon Bar on the main deck. Still getting acclimated? Enjoy duty-free shopping on our lower level. If it's food you want, sample our culinary delights at Food Lover's Paradise on level two. We've got mambo and margaritas at midnight. Fun and games start tomorrow, so if you need to sit one night out, we'll see you in the morning!"

Lenny had a look of panic on his face. "We can't take Homer through the common areas now. Too many people will see us." He looked wild-eyed. "I don't know what to do." He glanced at the railing and bit his lip as if deep in thought. That thought might have involved tossing Homer's body overboard, which, along with his wild, shifty eyes, I would also have filed under "guilty behavior."

"Our room," I said.

"What?" Tex and Lenny asked at the same time. One of them sounded incredulous, and the other sounded hopeful.

"I'm only up here because I wanted a chance to relax." I told Tex. "Willow said our new room wouldn't be ready for us until tomorrow, so our things are still in our original room on the second floor. From everything I've heard, that room is out of the way. You can put Homer's body there, and Tex and I can sleep in one of the vacant guest rooms tonight."

"What vacant guest rooms?" Tex asked. "Homer said there was a rush of last-minute customers."

"Willow told me the cruise was only partially booked. That means there are vacant rooms."

"Willow was right," Lenny said. "By all estimations, the idea for this cruise was a turkey. We're only at half occupancy. We can put Homer in your old room. I'll notify the coast guard, and we'll arrange to hand off his body when we dock at Cozumel."

"Cozumel is in Mexico," I said, stating the obvious.

"You have to take him back to the States," Tex said.

Lenny's stage fright in the face of emergency heightened. "You mean we have to keep him on the ship?"

Tex turned to me. "Have you ever seen something like this on one of your true-crime TV shows?"

My heart pounded. Being on this ship represented a whole different set of rules when it came to a murder, and from the angle at which that knife had been sticking out of

Homer's chest, it would be difficult to call what happened to Homer anything else.

"I'm no expert, but Homer is a US citizen, right?"

"Right."

"Then I'm pretty sure you need to take his body back to the United States for a proper investigation into his death."

"But this is a five-day cruise. Doesn't something start to happen to bodies after, you know..." Lenny did *not* seem to want to state the obvious, and I didn't blame him.

"You'll have to keep him cold."

"There's a bathtub in your room," Lenny said somewhat helpfully. "The kitchen can send up ice."

With a plan in place, we moved quickly. I held the door to the staff entrance and checked for a clear coast while Tex and the boatswain carried Homer's body. The room was just about big enough for Homer, which made me wonder why Homer had thought it would work for me and Tex and my Doris Day wardrobe. Our luggage was stacked in the corner, suitcase on top of suitcase in a teetering heap, garment bag on top, with Tex's black nylon roller bag to the side.

At Tex's suggestion, the two men put Homer's body in the bathtub. Lenny closed the curtains in the room and cranked up the air conditioner. I stood in the doorway, acting as lookout when I wasn't watching the action in the room. Considering we were operating under the instructions of a person in authority, it felt an awful lot like aiding and abetting a criminal.

Lenny pulled a key card out of his pocket and handed it to Tex. "This is my master passkey. It'll get you into any room on the ship. Whatever you do, don't lose it. Room three-oh-seven is vacant. I'll come find you later and swap it out with a regular key card, but there's no time now."

"What about our luggage?" I asked.

"We're only staying in three-oh-seven tonight," Tex said. "It doesn't make sense to move our luggage twice."

"We still need pajamas."

Tex gave me a typical Tex look.

"*I* still need pajamas."

Tex grinned.

"I can't risk asking someone to move your luggage from this room," Lenny said. "Take what you need now. I'll have the rest moved to your new room when I can free someone up."

I went back into the tiny room and shivered. The air-conditioning was already working overtime, and the room was cool. Goose bumps sprang up on my arms and legs. There was no point in unpacking my one suitcase just to repack it in the morning, so I flipped open two suitcases before finding the one with my overnight things. I removed my bathing suit and cover-up, too, and grabbed a garment bag.

Tex waited for me in the hallway.

"Aren't you taking anything?" I asked him.

"I have everything I need."

"Where's Lenny?"

"He got called away." Tex held his finger up to his lips. "You ready?"

"Let's go."

Our first two hours on the cruise ship were more eventful than I'd expected of the entire cruise, and that included the activities on the entertainment schedule. We made up for the unexpected rash of activity over the next two hours, when we fell asleep in our second room of the day.

"Mmmmmmmmmm." Tex rolled over and slung his arm across me.

"Not now, Mr. Templeton." I grabbed his wrist and moved his arm then sat up.

It was going on eight o'clock. My last meal had been breakfast, and I was hungry. I roused Tex to see if he was interested in dinner.

"I'm interested in food but not in dinner."

"Meaning what?"

"Dinner is going to be a production. People expect you to mingle. Which is good, because you'll be able to ask questions that seem innocent, and you might find something out."

"Surely you don't still expect us to investigate Nasty's crime ring?"

"Of course I do. She hired us to do a job."

"She hired us to find out who on the crew was stealing from the guests. I found a body with a knife sticking out of it. The picture has changed."

Tex rolled onto his side and propped on his elbow. "To what?"

"We are no longer innocently snooping around to expose a cat burglar. There's a murderer on the cruise ship."

"How do you know Homer wasn't the cat burglar? Maybe someone caught him in the act."

"And stabbed him? That seems rash."

"Not if he threatened them first."

"Self-defense," I said. I considered that for a moment. "I suppose that could have been the case. But if you accidentally murdered someone in self-defense, would you flee the scene?"

"Most people who murder someone flee the scene,

accidental or not. But maybe that's not it. Maybe Homer caught the burglar in the act."

"And the burglar killed Homer to keep him from exposing them?"

"Could be."

"It could have been his partner," I said. "A double cross."

"Sure. Too bad you didn't see anybody in the area."

"Lenny showed up pretty quickly. He could have been there already. And what about Jennifer?"

"Who?"

"The mermaid. Don't you think it's suspicious that she was in the water right then? She could have stabbed Homer and then pulled on a mermaid tail and dived into the water to give her an alibi. Even Lenny said nobody knows when she does her thing. It's a pretty good cover." I tapped my lips with my fingertip. "And you can't count out Meg and Mavis."

"Who are Meg and Mavis?"

Silly me. I almost didn't notice the subtlety with which Tex encouraged me to keep hypothesizing.

"The Stork sisters. You'll know them when you see them. They're two Black women dressed in pink and aqua. At least, today they are. They told me they're cruise regulars, so they know a thing or two about the cruise. They know the ship, they know the schedule, and they said they always spend the first day of a cruise in their room to get acclimated. Maybe they didn't. Maybe that was a lie to make people think they were indisposed while the—" I turned to Tex, fully prepared to share more theories, when I saw the smile on his face. "What?" I crossed my arms.

"I don't have to investigate Nasty's crime ring. You're doing a bang-up job for the both of us."

CHAPTER SEVEN

It was decided. Mr. and Mrs. Templeton would not be getting off the cruise ship at the first port of call.

As Tex deftly pointed out, the crime might have changed, but the job remained the same. I secretly wondered if Nasty knew more about the criminal activities she'd hired us to investigate than she'd said at our interview. Nasty was good at her job, but she had a sliding moral compass that allowed her to get what she wanted without always playing by the rules. I admired her ability to flourish in a man's world while I also occasionally begrudged her sex appeal. She indeed had it both ways.

She also had a little boy. Huxley was the result of a questionable dalliance between Nasty and Gerry Rose, one of Dallas's ten wealthiest men, who also happened to be in his seventies. Nasty claimed Gerry understood her in a way single men her age did not, and she'd shocked us all by refusing to marry him when he proposed. She'd wanted nothing from him except his sperm. Huxley was hers and hers alone.

Huxley was two and a half years old, and a two-and-a-half-year-old was not something to leverage into a cover story on a cruise ship with a criminal. Nasty got results, but even I knew she wouldn't put her little boy at risk to do so.

Was it comforting to know Nasty thought of Tex and me as expendable? About as comforting as it was to know she thought we could get the job done. On the grand seesaw of perspective, I focused on the latter.

Our first room, the one currently occupied by Homer's body, had been a closet with a porthole view of the ocean. Today's lodgings were comparatively palatial. It had two queen beds, a desk, a sliding door, and a balcony with two chairs. Tex had opened the sliding doors when we first entered, and salty ocean air filled the room. The last thing I thought I would notice while cruising to Cozumel was the sea air, so I was pleasantly surprised by how refreshing it felt. I stood by the doors and inhaled deeply, then exhaled, and pushed thoughts of the murder and thieving cruise employees out of my mind. For the first time since arriving, I decompressed. The trip didn't have to be all stress. I could find ways to enjoy it.

"When's your first performance?" Tex asked.

And the stress was back.

While Tex stretched out in the middle of the bed, I searched my luggage for my itinerary. Unfortunately, the location of my itinerary soon became clear. "My itinerary is in one of my other bags. They're still in the room with Homer." I sat on the edge of the bed. "Give me the passkey, and I'll go back and get it."

Tex pulled a folded-up sheet of paper out of his back pocket. He held it out.

I took the page and smoothed it over the bedspread. It was our itinerary. "I'm impressed."

"I told you I had everything I needed. You're welcome."

"When you said that, I thought you were implying something else."

"I was." Tex laced his fingers together and rested his head on his hands. "But my schedule is flexible. I can wait."

Tex occasionally appeared to have a one-track mind, but I'd long ago learned that the illusion was fostered to work in his favor. His mind was always going in five different directions: assessing crime scenes, overseeing the police department, training new hires, gauging the veracity of suspect statements, and yes, checking out women. He was no saint. Tex wasn't just the captain of the Lakewood Police Department, a position he'd gotten a few years ago after being under suspicion himself, but he was also their top man. And it was a good thing, too, because crime was on the rise, and the department needed people to multitask more than ever.

Nasty and Tex had a complicated relationship. Scratch that. Nasty and Tex had a streamlined relationship. After dating, living together briefly, and breaking up, they'd reached a point of professional respect. Her work as the owner of a security company had helped Tex out more than once. And as much as Nasty and I had started out as adversaries, she'd proven to be one of the most reliable people I'd ever met, saving me a time or two. When she'd asked us to take on this job, it wasn't just a favor for a friend. It was a debt come due, disguised as a free cruise vacation. Nasty was crafty that way.

I scanned the activities outlined on the paper. A bigger cruise would have scheduled multiple happenings at the same time, but the *New Nautilus* didn't have the accommodations or staff to manage multiple ways to fritter away time. The schedule was lined out neatly: yoga at sunup, shuffleboard court open at ten, poolside bingo after lunch, and "top-notch entertainment" at night. Several late-night activities were marked as No Phone to keep the experience as close to nature as possible.

The ship had two restaurants—one a buffet, one a sit-down establishment—both open for breakfast, brunch, lunch, and dinner. Snacks were available at the poolside bar. The main pool was open round the clock, as was the observatory deck on the bottom level. A glass-bottom viewing station was described as part of the fun. I couldn't imagine Jennifer in her mermaid suit swimming underneath the ship, but I was curious enough that I wanted to see the glass bottom for myself.

That night, being the first night of the cruise, had a light schedule. The main activity was Meet & Mingle on the Mezzanine, which spanned several hours, followed by margaritas and mambo lessons at midnight. Somebody liked alliteration.

I was temporarily off the hook, a fact I shared with Tex. "The Meet and Mingle has been going on since we departed. If we divide and conquer, we can probably get a big-picture view of the rest of the people on board and suss out anybody acting suspiciously."

"Or you can do the meet and greet while I snoop."

"Meet and Mingle."

"Same diff." He held the boatswain's passkey between his fingers and flipped it over his knuckles in the same way gangsters flipped poker chips in old movies. "Lenny's going to expect this back as soon as he works out the room situation, but for now, I can come and go as I please."

"You can't be serious. Aren't you worried about walking in on someone?"

"The meet and mingle is too perfect of an opportunity. These people paid to be a part of this voyage. They're not going to hide in their rooms."

I remembered Meg and Mavis Stork. "Some are taking today to acclimate to the feeling of being on a boat."

"I've got one day to accidentally walk into the wrong room. After tonight, that's going to be suspicious. I'll take my chances to see what I can find out."

"I guess that means I'm off to work the crowd."

I went into the bathroom and checked my reflection. Genetics had given me Doris Day's perky nose, her expressive eyes, and when I laughed, her wide, engaging smile. Lifelong dedication to sunscreen had kept me looking a lot younger than my five decades, but it provided the biggest difference between me and my favorite actress. I lacked the glowing tan and freckles she sported. That and my hair color, more ashy than blond thanks to an encroaching quantity of gray.

I opened my train case and got to work. To prep for the trip, I'd had my shoulder-length blond hair cut into a style similar to Doris Day in the late sixties: chin-length with bangs. I sprayed dry shampoo into my hair to thicken it and raked my fingers through it to get it to fall into place. I tied a thick piece of yellow yarn in a bow above my bangs. It was a hairstyle Doris Day had worn regularly on her TV show, later than the years I was representing. I hoped the audience wouldn't criticize my choice too much.

Freckles were a little harder—but not impossible—to

come by. I pulled a fresh toothbrush out of my train case and coated the bristles in liquid bronzer. I put on a rubber glove and dragged my finger over the bristles while holding the brush next to my face. The bronzer spattered onto the bridge of my nose. I'd picked up the technique from a YouTube makeup tutorial filmed by a millennial influencer. I misted on setting spray to keep my new freckles in place then swiped on a fresh coat of Revlon Moon Drops lipstick in Apple Polish. Doris wore this shade for forty years before it was discontinued. Over the years, I'd come into possession of a lot of partially used cosmetics good for nothing but the packaging. Occasionally, I bought out the estate of a woman who had found her signature shade of lipstick and stockpiled it. Those unopened tubes went into a Tupperware container in my refrigerator to prolong their life.

I tucked the tube of lipstick into my pocket for touch-ups. When I came out of the bathroom, Tex sat on the bed. He glanced at me then did a double take.

"Geez, Night, you look like June."

"June who?"

"On your Doris Day calendar. You look like June. That picture of her in the red outfit with the knee socks."

"Since when do you look at my Doris Day calendar?"

"I had to check your schedule."

"For what?"

"It's not important."

I crossed my arms. "Maybe I should be the judge of that."

Before we had a chance to litigate the matter, the phone rang. Since neither Tex nor I was expecting a phone call, and since nobody on the boat should have been expecting anyone to be in room 307, we stared at the phone while it rang.

"Do we answer?" I asked.

"It could be Lenny. He's the one who put us here. Answer it."

"Why me?"

"You're the reason we're on this boat. If someone is calling the Templetons, they're calling you."

I picked up the phone and held the receiver to my ear. The line was crackly and distorted. I was about to say hello when a voice spoke. "Be careful. I think there's a cop on board the ship."

"Who is this?" I asked.

The call disconnected.

CHAPTER EIGHT

I STOOD FACING THE GRASS CLOTH WALLPAPER, HOLDING THE receiver up even after the dial tone sounded in my ear.

"We have a problem."

"What?"

"Whoever that was just said there was a cop on board the ship." I studied Tex's expression, trying to get a read on what he was thinking, before I shared the last piece of information.

"Not possible."

"You're a cop, and you're on the boat. It's not only possible, but also true."

"That's not what I meant. It's not possible that someone knows I'm a cop unless Nasty leaked it, and Nasty wouldn't leak it."

"Wouldn't she?"

We stared at each other. There was one truth we'd accepted when we took this job, and it was that we were working for Nasty. The problem with that "truth" was that Nasty had her own agenda. I didn't doubt that we were working for her, but I started to question whether the job we were hired to do was to expose a crime ring or create a distraction.

"What are you going to do?" I asked Tex.

"Nothing." He held out the passkey to me. "At least right now. I need to think about what this means. In the meantime, I might seem suspicious, but you don't. Not a single person on this boat will assume you are anything other than what you are. You'll need to handle the covert aspects of this mission."

If the situation weren't so dire, I would have laughed.

Tex continued. "I probably don't have to say this, but I will anyway. That call makes it sound like our burglary ring is still operational. The murder of the entertainment director may be an entirely unrelated crime."

I took the passkey and slipped it into one of my dress pockets. "What you're saying is for me to be careful."

"Be careful," he repeated. "And don't blow your cover. Until I figure something out, you're Nasty's only operational asset on this boat."

I kissed Tex goodbye and left.

I would have liked to become familiar with the layout of the boat, but the *New Nautilus* had been under renovation, and the old diagrams were outdated. I walked down the hall, taking note of wall-mounted signs that pointed toward guest rooms, restaurants, elevators, and stairs. Nasty was right about the effects of being out on the ocean. The inflammation had almost entirely left my bad knee, and I felt nimbler than I had in ages. I practically owned stock in Keds thanks to the number of CVOs in my wardrobe, but for the cruise, I'd packed an assortment of low-heeled pumps to go with my performance wardrobe.

Signs directed me to the stairs, which led me to the mezzanine, which held a crowd of people holding colorful cocktails. This was it. My last chance to turn around and hide.

"Doris! Yoo-hoo! Over here!"

I scanned the crowd. Mavis Stork flapped her hand to get my attention. Her beverage was a shade similar to her outfit, frothy blue with a yellow umbrella. I knew it was Mavis, because she was still dressed in her aqua ensemble, and I'd made the connection between the *a* in aqua and the *a* in Mavis. It was a twenty-four-hour solution to one of my lesser problems.

"Mavis," I said. A waiter handed me a flute of champagne. I clinked glasses with Mavis and took a sip. Bubbles tickled my nose. "Where is your sister?"

"She's in the room, the poor thing. Always gets sick the first day of a cruise. If she gets it under control, she might join me later for mambo lessons. Now me, I take Dramamine. Helps with the adjustment. I don't like missing out on any of the action." She took another swig of her aqua drink. "Where's Rock?"

"Rock?" I repeated. "Oh, I forgot you were there when I got that phone call. He's fine. A little chapped at how things worked out, but he'll forget all about it the second a distraction crosses his path."

Mavis's face fell. "He's not mad at you, is he? For being the main attraction? Some males get so jealous."

"No, he's very understanding about things like this."

Mavis apparently found that fascinating. "You're not worried he'll take advantage of having so much time to himself?"

"I'll call him from time to time. He's used to waiting for the phone to ring."

Mavis took another sip of her drink, that time a little more cautiously. I pulled out another Doris Day expression and forced a laugh. "He'll be fine. Even dogs deserve a little freedom now and then."

Mavis spit her blue drink back into her glass. I handed her my cocktail napkin, and she dabbed her mouth and the front of her shirt where a few errant drops had landed.

"Would you excuse me?" she asked. "I should go check on my sister." Before I had a chance to answer, she hurried past me.

If that interaction was any indication, I was going to have to adjust my small talk. I finished my champagne, and a waiter handed me a second flute. Working a crowd while pretending to be someone I wasn't was far from how I usually spent my time, and the alcohol relaxed me just enough to do my job. I thanked the waiter and moved through the crowd, saying "hello" here and "nice to see you" there. Most people were more interested in talking among themselves than to the stranger pretending to be America's original sweetheart. As I came out the other side of the crowd, I stood next to two men in golf shirts. Neither looked happy to see me.

"Hello," I said. "Are you enjoying your departure day?"

The first man shook his head. "Our girlfriends are travel agents. We're only here because the tickets were cheap."

"They didn't tell us it was a nostalgia cruise," the second man said.

The first man took a moment to scan me from head to toe. "No offense, but this isn't really our thing."

"What *is* your thing?" It seemed the polite question.

"Golf," they said in unison.

"I heard there's a putting range on the ship."

"There was. They removed it to make room for an art gallery."

"That's a shame." It was the second time someone had mentioned the renovations, and it seemed an odd choice to remove one of the most popular activities on the boat for something that had nothing to do with the 1966 theme. "Are your girlfriends around?"

"Mine's talking to Mick Jagger. His is with Keith Richards." He pointed across the deck at a thin man with shaggy hair and big lips. He wore a striped T-shirt and bell-bottoms. He chatted with a woman in a sparkly gold dress.

"Aren't you jealous?"

The man laughed. "Are you kidding? I slipped Mick a twenty to take her off my hands."

The second man had been quiet while his buddy talked. In the back of my mind, I was aware of the fact that to commit the crimes I was trying to expose, a person would likely have a partner. These two men were perfect partners, as would be one of them and his wife. Any one person on the ship could be half of a crime ring, and that complicated things.

As did the murder.

It was easy to conclude the two were connected. That meant someone had upgraded their criminal activity from misdemeanor to felony. Perhaps one crime had begotten the other. Maybe it was self-defense or a spontaneous act when one partner realized he could double his profits with a single act of violence. The other possibility was the odd coincidence of a murder and a burglary ring coexisting on the same cruise. That felt far-fetched but not impossible. We were out to sea, and that meant different laws, different jurisdiction, and a different punishment for crimes committed. It was a unique environment for a criminal to operate in, and it might have been that very environment that attracted the criminal kind. Maybe cruises were already a hotbed of illegal activity and I'd just never known it.

A waiter approached me and topped off my second glass of champagne. The first flute relaxed me and bridged my awkwardness at working the room, but the second glass, on top of my not having eaten since we departed, left me lightheaded. I didn't need more. I smoothed my hand over my dress and felt the flat rectangular key card in my pocket. Perhaps it was the appropriate time to excuse myself and open a few doors.

CHAPTER NINE

THE COAST WAS, IN FACT, CLEAR. I ROUNDED THE CORNER ON my way to the stairs and passed a ballroom. Two steps past it, I stopped and backtracked until I stood in the doorway. A woman in overalls and a T-shirt had her back to me. She stood on a drop cloth, staring at an empty wall. Around her sat boxes of record albums, a glue gun, a hammer, and a drill. She didn't seem to know she had stepped into the loop of an electrical cord plugged into the wall and that if she took a step in any direction, it would most likely cause her to fall like the victim of a Wile E. Coyote trap. Seeing the potential accident about to happen, I entered the ballroom and called out, "Be careful!"

The woman whipped around and looked at me. "You can't be in here," she said. She started to head my way, and the electrical cord tightened around her ankle. With her next step, the cord tugged her back. She glanced down and kicked a few times to free herself, to no avail.

"Don't move," I instructed. I went into the room and

pointed at her foot. "You're tangled up. I'll free you." On any other day, dropping onto my knees would take a little more effort, but with the inflammation in my bad knee gone, I felt like I could do anything. I squatted and untangled the cord from her ankle then stood. "I've gotten twisted up in a cord hundreds of times. God bless the person who invented cordless tools."

"You're the vocalist, aren't you?" she asked.

"Yes. I'm Madison, but you can call me Doris if that's what's expected."

"Nobody expects you to go by Doris unless you're performing." The woman looked down at the drop cloth and kicked the cord farther away from her foot. She looked up at me and narrowed her eyes. "If you're a singer, why do you use power tools?"

In my mind, I replayed what I'd just said. In a clumsy attempt to protect my cover, I said, "I meant the microphone cord."

She narrowed her eyes. "You said cordless *tools*."

"I meant power tools for you. For me, it's a cordless mic." To sell my cover story, I pantomimed holding a microphone.

"Yeah, well, like I said, you can't be in here." The woman seemed to buy my clumsy attempt at a cover story. She slipped a bandana that had been knotted around her neck up to her head to hold her loose hair back. "I'm Persephone. I'd love to stand around and chat, but the ballroom needs to be ready for tomorrow, and I'm trying to make something out of nothing. And now, thanks to Homer, I'm running behind."

The absence of a *thank you* did not go unnoticed. Nor did the dig about standing around and talking, which seemed a little hostile considering I'd just rescued her from a spill. The making-something-out-of-nothing comment was like catnip to my decorating side, but at the mention of Homer, the now-deceased purser, my attention shifted to that.

"What do you know about Homer?"

"Only that he was supposed to help me get this room decorated. He said he had a plan, but then he didn't show. Now I've got a bunch of boxes from somebody's garage and a room that needs to be transformed by tomorrow night. I shouldn't be surprised. He volunteered to help me when we were—" Her cheeks flushed pink, and even though she didn't finish her sentence, I had a good idea what she and Homer had been. "But now we're not. I should have thought about my job before—" She glanced at me.

I found her every word riveting, not just because she spoke with animation. My interest might have shown on my face.

"Whatevs. He's not my problem anymore."

It wasn't my place to tell her what had happened to Homer if, in fact, she didn't know. But if I did tell her, I wondered whether she would backpedal and show regret over her callous words or stand by them. I assumed Lenny would notify the captain about the murder and that the captain would notify the employees. I figured when that happened, the news would eventually trickle to me from someone chatty. For the moment, like Tex said, *mum's the word.*

"Maybe I can help you," I offered.

"No offense, but you're the entertainment, right? The insurance policy alone precludes you from lifting anything over five pounds. Don't you have to get ready for some cruise ship activity?"

"Not today. I just came from the Meet and Mingle Mixer on the mezzanine, which is breaking up as people head for cocktails." I stepped back and assessed the elements scattered on the floor around her. "Let's pretend the insurance policy doesn't exist. I can spare a few minutes if you want a separate set of hands."

"Do you want me to get fired? If anybody hears I asked the talent to help me decorate the nightclub, I won't even get a return trip to Galveston. I'm already in trouble over the putting range."

"I thought the putting range was removed."

"Right. I was told to build a movie-viewing room. Something about showing Doris Day movies on a loop. Now I find out we have more golfers than movie fans."

"I heard you removed it to make room for an art gallery."

"You might want to check your source."

The longer I talked to Persephone, the more I sensed she wanted me to leave. I'd done nothing to offend her, and my suspicion radar was on high alert. For someone who was where she should be, she was acting more hostile than necessary.

The erroneous information about the renovation had come to me via the two golfers who'd been dragged along on the trip by their girlfriends, and I tried to remember what else they had said. It was one thing to get a few details wrong, especially if you regularly tuned out your girlfriends as those two had appeared to do. But was it just them not paying attention, or was their misinformation misdirection?

"Does that mean there's no movie-viewing room?"

"It depends. If enough people complain about the putting range, I'll have to find some other corner of the ship to convert."

Despite the fact that I'd kept her talking, I couldn't help but detect an us-versus-you tone. She didn't view me as one of the employees on the *New Nautilus*. I was part of the problem.

I felt the effects of the champagne. My head thudded, and my throat was dry. I glanced at the clock, which had been removed from the wall and now sat on the edge of her drop cloth. Only about five minutes remained until time for the mixer, and if any passengers had too much to drink, they might retire to their rooms instead of going straight to dinner. I had excused myself so I could snoop, but thanks to the current distraction, I was losing my window of opportunity.

"I should be getting on my way." I suddenly had an idea. "But my husband is on the boat, and he doesn't have any official duties except as my companion. No insurance policy for him. If a second set of hands would help, I'm sure he'd pitch in."

"Sure," Persephone said dismissively. "If he's just your husband, he's nobody important. I guess it's too much to ask if he knows anything about decorating."

"He knows his way around a sputnik lamp." I winked.

"Did you get something in your eye?"

"No, but you're installing a 1966 theme, right? I meant he recognizes items from the atomic era. Sputnik lamps, Plattner tables, Eames chairs. The classics."

I made the first reference to be friendly. The second round exaggerated Tex's knowledge of my decorating forte, but he'd picked up a few things since spending time with me. It wasn't every day I met someone who specialized in the same era that I did, and I would have loved to toss aside my cover story and chat with the woman about bow tie sconces and butterfly roofs. But as I ran through a list of the most well-known designs to come out of the mid-century aesthetic, one thing became clear—the supposed mid-century modern expert decorator on board the ship had no idea what I was talking about.

Persephone pulled out a device like the one Willow had used. "Let me scan your key card so I can find your room."

"It's three-oh-seven," I said quickly.

"That can't be. That's the vacant wing."

"My room assignment is temporary. I wasn't happy with our original room. Lenny is working on getting me new accommodations, but I don't know what they'll be. Let me see if there's been a change."

I turned around and looked for a phone. One was mounted to the wall just inside the entrance. I walked over to it, pretending everything was cool. I picked up the receiver and dialed 3-0-7. The phone rang. And rang. And rang. Tex didn't seem to be in the room.

The problem with Tex not answering was that now, it looked like our room had changed, and that meant our key card would have been updated with the new room number. I couldn't pull out the passkey, not without raising suspicion, so I pretended Tex answered.

"Hi," I said to the ringing phone. "It's me. I was just checking to see if you're still in the room. I was on my way there, but I got waylaid." I stopped talking for a moment to make it seem as if someone had responded.

And someone did, just not from the phone.

"Waylaid?" Tex said behind me. "Sounds like fun."

I whirled around with the receiver clutched in my hand. My eyes were wide, as if I'd been caught with my hand in the cookie jar. I set the receiver back on the cradle without saying goodbye to the imaginary participant in my phantom conversation.

"Who are you?" Persephone asked.

Tex didn't know I wasn't alone in the room, and Persephone's voice clearly surprised him. "I'm her husband, Tex Templeton."

CHAPTER TEN

ONE MISSISSIPPI. TWO MISSISSIPPI. THREE MISSISSIPPI.

I counted the beats, the long, awkward seconds that stretched as Persephone processed the fact that I couldn't have been talking to my husband in our room if my husband was there with us. She looked from his face to mine then back to his. She strode forward and held out her hand.

"Hi. I'm Persephone, the ship decorator. Your wife volunteered you to pull an all-nighter with me."

That wasn't exactly what I'd volunteered, but I let things play out. Tex didn't miss a beat.

"She's just trying to keep me busy while she has fun on the cruise. You know what divas are like." He winked at her. Funny, she didn't ask *him* if he had something in his eye.

Tex lowered his brows slightly. His ability to gauge my body language was like putting a strip of litmus paper into a chemical and coming up with a positive result. I pressed my lips together and forced a smile. Persephone couldn't see Tex, but she was still watching me. From everything she'd heard already, I was the one with something to hide.

"Why don't you two work out details? I'm going to go relax in our room." I pulled the passkey out of my pocket, and Tex nodded.

I left the two of them in the ballroom and headed down the hall and around the corner. The whole point of me being out and about was to snoop, and I'd wasted valuable time with a decorating distraction.

The décor of the boat continued to be a distraction but not in the way I would have liked. The carpet was dark blue with a pattern of white seashells. The walls of the boat were smooth aluminum. An occasional generic print of a lighthouse or fishing boat was mounted to the walls at not-quite-even intervals, no apparent logic behind the choice of work or the arrangement of subject matter. Even the lights were an afterthought. They looked as if they'd come straight out of a lighting store running a discount sale on bulk purchases. I wanted to rip it all down and start over, but that wasn't my job.

Signs directed me up a short flight of stairs to guest quarters. I looked to my left and my right and scanned the key card on the first door. The light by the lock changed from red to green, and I heard a *click*.

I pushed the door open and tentatively stepped inside. The room was similar to the one Tex and I were temporarily holed up in. It had two queen beds, each covered in a peach-and-aqua bedspread printed with large fish. A closed suitcase sat on the luggage cart by the sliding doors. I peeked inside the bathroom and spotted a red canvas overnight kit on the sink. It was still zipped.

Nothing about the room seemed suspicious or amiss, and apart from rooting through a stranger's luggage, which felt like going one step too far, I didn't know what else I might find out by being there. I backed out and moved on to the next room, finding a similar scene. This time it was three rolling suitcases in various shades of blue lined up next to each other by the foot of the beds.

The third room indicated a female guest who had unpacked and hung a collection of colorful muumuus in the closet. The fourth room held T-shirts and cargo shorts that had already been organized in drawers. The fifth had a king bed, and the sixth had several empty beer cans in the trash. I reached the end of the hallway feeling as if I'd either missed some key piece of evidence or wasted time in this hall, then I heard footsteps. I turned around and found myself face-to-face with Meg in her head-to-toe pink.

"Hi, Madison!" she said cheerfully.

"Shouldn't you call me Doris?"

She waved off the notion. "Don't pay attention to Mavis. She's a stickler when it comes to celebrity cruises. She's probably the only person here who will call you Doris Day."

"But you—"

"I go along with her." She smiled. "What are you doing in this hall? Your room isn't around here, is it? The talent usually gets a room near the ballroom."

"I was… just taking a walk. Getting acclimated with the layout of the ship."

"This isn't your first cruise, is it?"

"It is."

She clapped. "A newbie! Does Mavis know? She's going to be so excited. We always try to meet the first-timers. You didn't tell her yet, did you?"

"I don't think I mentioned it."

"How could you? You didn't say anything when we first

met you, and poor Mavis, she's been resting in the room since we arrived."

If I hadn't already been on high alert for suspicious behavior, I might not have picked up on the fact that both sisters indicated the other was taking the first day of the cruise to get acclimated. At best, each was being polite. At worst, the volunteered information was a red flag.

As innocent as Meg and Mavis seemed, no one on the ship was above a second look. Tex and I still didn't know if we had two crimes or if the burglaries and the murder were connected. If we had two, then the Stork sisters were as likely as anyone to be the thieves. And if not, well, I'd already rubbed a few of the employees the wrong way. It wouldn't hurt to have the cruise regulars on my side.

Meg and I stood in the hallway. The *thud* of footsteps coming toward us on the hall carpet mixed with laughter and conversation. Two couples rounded the corner, but it wasn't clear who was with whom until the two men unlocked one room and two women unlocked the other. I recalled the luggage inside each of those rooms. The women were in the room with the T-shirts and cargo shorts, and the men were in the room with the muumuus? I was going to have to keep an eye on them, because those four people did not match up with my initial assessment of them from their belongings.

I saw an opportunity to learn which room was Meg's, and I took it. "I don't mean to keep you from your quarters," I said. "We can walk and talk."

"I'm not going to my room yet, but I'll come with you to yours. You're on the lido deck, right?"

"Not anymo—yes." Meg should not have known which room was mine, and she shouldn't know that the boatswain had moved us into a temporary room while he arranged our final destination. I plunged my hand into my pocket and wrapped my fingers around Lenny's passkey. I could unlock any room on the boat, and right then, the safest one to unlock was the one I had no chance of occupying after all was said and done.

We walked side by side down the hall. Meg kept up a steady stream of chatter, covering the weather ("Did you see that blue sky this afternoon?"), the cruise company ("They could have done a better job promoting this"), the agenda ("Shuffleboard at sunset? Whose bright idea was that?"), and the décor ("peach-and-aqua bedspreads with a cobalt-blue carpet? The decorator should lose her license.")

I said just enough to seem engaged in the conversation, but quietly, I built a profile. Yes, I saw the blue sky, but I didn't mention I'd seen it from the deck where I'd also seen a body. Whoever had committed the crime had surely seen that blue sky as well. Her interest in shuffleboard stood out because the shuffleboard court was the crime scene. And the decorator, well, I had issues with Persephone's choices too.

I didn't know the boat well enough to lead Meg to my original room, but fortunately for me, she knew the way. We reached the end of the hallway, and she opened a door marked Exit.

Meg stood back and held the door open.

I hesitated before entering. The door opened onto a staircase, yes, but the bare walls and metal staircase indicated that this part of the ship was not intended for passengers. "Shouldn't we stick to the main parts of the ship?"

Meg turned and pointed the way we had come. "You can if you want, but you'll have to go back down the hallway, up to the mezzanine, past the art gallery, and down the other end of the hall to the grand staircase. There's a cruise photographer there for the next two hours, and people love having their portraits taken on the first day of the cruise. Once you get down the stairs, you'll have to head all the way back this way to get to your room."

"You know this ship really well," I observed.

She shrugged. "It pays to know the shortcuts."

She tipped her head toward the stairs, and I headed inside. I started down the stairs with my hand firmly on the banister. Even though my knee was feeling no pain, I went slowly. Meg was behind me, and it wasn't every day you met a woman in head-to-toe pastel pink and wondered whether she planned to shove you down a flight of stairs.

We reached the lower level, but before I was able to open the door, someone burst into the stairwell. It was Mavis. She seemed as surprised to see me as I was to see her.

"You'll never guess who's on board the ship!"

"Who?" Meg asked.

"Not a who, a *what*. A cosmonaut!" Mavis's eyes were wide, almost the same shade as her aqua shirt, which seemed so unnatural that I quickly attributed her eye color to colored contacts. She practically vibrated with enthusiasm. She grabbed her sister's arm and pulled her closer. "I followed him through the ship to find his room. He's staying right there." She pointed at the nearest door.

"That can't be," I said, because the door she pointed at went to my original room—the room that hid Homer's body.

"It's true," Mavis said. "He was a last-minute passenger, and he specifically requested a room on the lower level. He doesn't want anybody to know he's here, but I'm very good at getting people to talk about themselves." She smiled proudly.

"She's right," Meg said. "It's like a superpower."

"And after finding out what a dog your husband is," Mavis said to me, "I think you should have your own fun on the cruise."

"A dog?"

Mavis turned to Meg. "You should have heard the conversation they had. He was pouty about spending time in his room. Do you know she had to promise him that he'd get to chase girls later?"

"That's not what that conversation was about," I said. I looked back and forth between the two sisters while trying to remember my overheard conversation with Rocky. She'd asked if he was mad at me being the main attraction and I'd said—no, even dogs deserve a little freedom. Nobody on this boat knew I'd left my dog in Galveston. Mavis must have thought I was talking about Tex! I replayed what I could remember of our conversation and grinned at the confusion. No wonder Mavis had made a swift exit after that!

While it was clear Mavis had drawn her own conclusions about Tex and my marriage, I quickly knew that misunderstanding might work in our favor.

Mavis asked what she must have seen as a more pressing question. "Why are you two down here?"

"I'm walking Madison to her room," Meg said. She turned to me. "So cool! You're in the same hallway as an astronaut. Maybe you'll have a cruise fling."

"*Cos*monaut," Mavis corrected. "He's Russian, remember?"

A chill swept over me. The last thing I needed while sleuthing for Nasty on the cruise was having to deal with the advances of a Russian cosmonaut.

"Even better," said Meg, who had a different standard for what would make for a good cruise. "He probably won't stalk you when the cruise is over."

I didn't point out that I was on the cruise with Mr. Templeton, because there were far more pressing issues at hand. "Exciting!" I forced myself to smile and hoped the look on my face was more enthusiastic than deer-in-the-headlights.

Nasty had given us a copy of the crew manifest, but that seemed to be only a part of the picture. I didn't want to judge our Russian cosmonaut before I met him, but I did wonder how someone with space credentials would find himself on a 1966-themed cruise ship—and why.

"Which room is yours?" Meg asked.

The beauty of having Lenny's passkey was that it opened doors, and right then, that was the one thing I needed: an open door. I turned my back to my original room and held the passkey in front of the lock on the opposite side of the hall. The red light switched to green, and the door latch clicked. I pushed the door open an inch. "Thank you, ladies. I'll see you both later!"

"But—"

"Wait—"

I stepped inside the room and leaned against the door to make it shut and lock quickly. I remained there, not moving, and listened for the sounds of the sisters walking away.

"I thought she'd invite us in," Meg said.

"She probably left her clothes strewn all over the beds. Let's give her the benefit of the doubt." Mavis's voice suddenly squealed with enthusiasm. "Oh my God! You're here!"

"Ladies," said a male voice.

Of my growing list of problems, which included an unknown killer, an unchecked burglary ring, a hostile decorator, and a pending performance of Doris Day material, the biggest one was the fact that I knew that if I turned around and pressed my eye to the peephole to watch the scene unfolding in the hallway, the parties involved would hear me.

The second biggest problem was that I recognized the voice.

CHAPTER ELEVEN

"Nice to see you again, Captain. This is my sister, Meg."

The passenger formerly known as Tex Templeton responded. "Nice to meet you. But please don't use my title while we're on the ship. If anybody finds out who I am, this won't be the relaxing vacation I wanted."

"What should we call you?"

The worst possible thing for Tex to say was his name, and the only way for me to stop him from saying it was to shock him into silence.

I yanked the door open. It worked.

Tex stared at me. For the briefest moment, he looked scared. Meg and Mavis turned from me to Tex and back to me. Mavis said, "Captain, this is Madison Templeton. She's the Doris Day impersonator. You two will probably get to know each other very well. She's in the room right across the hall from you."

Tex's expression settled into one I recognized, and it wasn't surprise or fear. It was opportunity. He leaned to the left, seeming to peer into my room. "Convenient," he said.

I reached behind me and pulled the door closed with force, relaxing against it after the *click* of the lock. I adopted my best Doris Day voice. "Nice to meet you." I glanced at the Stork sisters, who might as well have ordered popcorn to eat while taking in the show. "Mavis here is right. We'll probably be seeing a lot of each other while on the ship."

"I certainly hope so." Tex raised his eyebrows suggestively, and Meg grinned, delighted to witness what she probably thought was our meet-cute.

"Come on, Meg," Mavis said. She hooked her arm in her sister's. "Let's head back to the lobby and have our departure pictures taken."

Mavis steered her sister to the stairs. As the door closed behind them, I heard one say, "That was just like a movie."

If Meg and Mavis had followed the carpeted hallway in the opposite direction from the stairs, I would have had no idea where they were after they rounded the corner. But the staircase was metal and fiberglass, and the sounds of flip-flops and voices bounced off the walls as they reached the next level above us. Neither Tex nor I spoke until the hallway and staircase were silent again, at which point I turned to him.

"You're an *astronaut?*"

"I'm Russian. They're cosmonauts."

"That doesn't make this better."

"I can explain."

"I'm sure you can, but you never have in the past, so why start now?"

"For starters, as long as we're on this boat, you're my partner."

Tex and I had never found ourselves in this position before. In the past, we'd come at his homicide investigations from two angles: he was the police presence investigating the crime, and I was the innocent bystander who happened to gain access to his crime scenes. He usually dissuaded me from getting involved in his cases, and I usually argued that I never tried to get involved, but in the course of doing my business, I happened to get involved, and when his cases bled into my life, I wasn't willing to walk away.

But thanks to Nasty, we were both responsible for the outcome of the current investigation. That meant we had to cooperate or fail in our job.

Our *mission*.

"Your room or mine?" I asked.

"I'm not sure," Tex said. "What were you doing in that room?"

"Meg—the one in the pink—wanted to walk me to my room, and she already seemed to know where it was. She led me here. When her sister showed up and said there was a cosmonaut in my old room, I used Lenny's passkey to let me into this one." I pointed at my room.

"Good thinking."

"You next."

Tex rubbed his hands over his head. "I left Persephone and was walking through the hallway when a call came in from the precinct."

"What precinct?"

"*My* precinct. Lakewood Police Department. Somebody broke into the equipment room. They stole the parking department's boots and have been going around the city booting cars."

"For what reason?"

"Practical joke, it seems. I'll take it. Beats the heck out of murders."

We were teetering on the edge of the day-to-day responsibilities of Tex's job as police captain versus mine as decorator, and as important as my business was to me, I tended to come out on the losing end of that comparison. Before he distracted me by listing the difficulties of his job, I kept him on track. "You took a call."

"Right. I thought I was alone, so I answered the way I always do."

"Captain Allen."

"Right. I said 'Captain' then realized what I did. I looked around and saw that lady in the aqua. I went the other direction and got the information I needed from Imogene. I didn't think anything of it until she cornered me."

"She's a middle-aged Doris Day fan. How, exactly, did she get you to crack?" It was only partially a joke. When Tex was in cop mode, he was remarkably stoic. I wouldn't have minded some pointers for the future.

"She asked what I did for a living. I couldn't remember if she knew I was with you or not, and I thought it might benefit us if I kept our identities separate. But before I had an answer, she asked if she could guess. She said she heard me identify myself as captain, and she started running through a list of possible captains. Army, Navy, Air Force, Marines, Coast Guard."

"She didn't guess police?"

"Nope."

"Is that suspicious? Somebody thinks there's a cop on board, remember?"

"If that was her, then she's a good actress. She listed every branch of the military. I thought she'd get bored, so I let her continue. When she got to the Space Force, I said astronaut."

"Cosmonaut."

Tex held up his hand. "I said *astronaut*. She said she had a cousin who works for NASA, and maybe I know him? She pulled out her phone like she was going to call him, and I said no, I was with a different space agency."

"How many space agencies do you think there are?"

"Space is a growth industry. I thought I could be vague and get out of there."

"I get the feeling Meg and Mavis Stork do not do 'vague.'"

"You're right about that." He chuckled. "She promised to keep my secret, and she asked my name."

"What did you tell her?"

"I didn't say Captain Allen, if that's your concern."

"It's one of many." I crossed my arms and tapped my foot, waiting for a response. "What is your name, Captain?"

"Komarov. Vladimir Komarov."

"Do I know that name?"

"Bone up on your space history, Night. Komarov was the first astronaut to die in space." Tex had the good sense to look embarrassed. "I know two Russian cosmonauts. Komarov and Yuri Gagarin. Gagarin is too well-known."

"You know a third," I said, a vague reference to someone we'd encountered during the case where we met, "but I thank you for not bringing him into this. Aren't you worried that Mavis's cousin who works for NASA might know Komarov?"

"Least of our problems. You remember what happened when you tried to use your phone. The farther we get from Galveston, the weaker the signal. She shouldn't be able to ask him until we're back in Texas, and if we don't make it through this cruise alive, I might follow in Komarov's footsteps."

What had started as a favor to Nasty was quickly

becoming a dark comedy. I had three personas: Madison Night, Madison Templeton, and Doris Day. Tex had Tex Allen, Tex Templeton, and Captain Komarov. For a party of two, our room was getting crowded.

"You know, there's something funny about those sisters." I left Tex standing in the hallway and went to the staircase. I pushed the exit door open and looked up at the cavernous emergency stairs, listening for sounds that someone was still there. The hallway was quiet. I stepped back and let the door fall into place. "Meg said her sister was resting in their room. But you said her sister was the one who approached you."

"Right. She told me her sister was the one who was indisposed."

It didn't take Tex's fictional rocket science degree to confirm that one of them was lying.

CHAPTER TWELVE

In the earliest instructions Nasty had given us after we agreed to take this job, she said every person on the cruise was a suspect. Initially, I took that to mean the crew. Not even a day in, we had a dead body and more persons of interest than I could count—each with opportunity. The one thing we didn't have was a theft. We were here to investigate a crime that had yet to occur.

"Unlock the door, Night," Tex said.

"Not that I don't love your charming habit of calling me by my last name, but don't you think your negligence has done enough to put our cover at risk?"

Tex pointed at the room across the hall from our original room. "Unlock the door, Templeton." He grinned.

I turned to the door and reached into my pockets. They were empty. I patted myself down. No passkey. "I think I dropped the key card."

"Where?"

I pointed at the door. "I was inside the room, so it must have been in there."

"What were you just saying about negligence?" Tex dropped to his hands and knees and peered under the bottom of the door. "It's on the carpet."

"Can you reach it?"

He stuck his fingers under the door. "No. I need a hanger or something."

There was one place to get a hanger or something, and that was in our original room across the hall. The creepy factor about entering our original room was that Homer's body was there too. But all things considered, Homer was the least-threatening person on the cruise. I held out my palm, and Tex slapped our original key card onto it. I went inside.

Thanks to the blasted air-conditioning, entering the room felt like walking into a meat locker. The door to the bathroom was closed like we'd left it. Lenny must have been there since we'd brought Homer's body because our luggage was gone. I went to the closet for a hanger, but the only ones there were the kind that couldn't be removed. It took me a moment of searching to come up with a pen, a postcard, and a room service menu.

I carried all three items to Tex. "No hanger."

Another person might have assumed I was hungry, but Tex had the MacGyver gene and assumed correctly that those were his raw materials for problem-solving. He took the room service menu and bent the edge then slipped it under the door and raked the passkey toward us. It was tedious work, but when we went to return the passkey, there would have been no way to explain to Lenny why I was inside a room that wasn't ours, so it was this or nothing.

Eventually, Tex got the key card close enough to the door

to slip his fingers underneath and pull it out. He stood, folded the menu, and put it in his pocket.

"Don't you want me to put it back?"

"Keepsake."

"Surely there's a more appropriate souvenir to represent this trip, *Captain*. Maybe we can find some moon rocks when we get to Cozumel."

Tex smiled but didn't respond. He used the passkey to unlock our original room. I waited in the hallway, and he rejoined me a few seconds later.

"We should find Lenny," Tex said. "Our luggage is gone, so he probably wants his key card back."

"I noticed that. I wasn't thrilled about the prospects of sharing the bathroom with Homer every time I have to touch up my freckles."

Tex didn't laugh. "I'm going to have to keep an eye on this room now that those sisters think I'm staying here."

"Better you than me."

Instead of taking the stairs, Tex and I went down the hallway and around the corner to the elevator. We'd been on the boat for about seven hours, and aside from our midday nap, it had been one thing after another. Every encounter, every incident, every happening had pointed out how out of place we were. Any number of people could have a secondary agenda designed to keep us distracted.

The biggest problem with *my* secondary agenda was that I had no real-life touchpoint to stabilize me. My decorating business back in Dallas—where I specialized in mid-century modern design, a self-taught specialty thanks to a lifetime of watching and rewatching Doris Day movies—was where I threw my energies when the rest of my life was in chaos. It was one thing to be on board the ship but another to be without a job to free up my mind. More than anything else, I was fidgety, and there was nothing in sight to settle my nerves.

Tex and I took advantage of our free time and retired to room 307. The phone rang, and I answered it nervously, unsure if our mystery caller was back.

"Mrs. Templeton? This is Lenny. If you and your husband can meet me at the luxury suites, we can swap out keys and you can settle in, but it's gotta be now. My other duties are backing up on me."

"Of course. Right. We'll be there as soon as we can." I hung up. "Time to rendezvous with Lenny."

"Are you going to milk the cosmonaut thing the whole time we're on the boat?"

"I'm leaning toward yes."

The only luggage we had with us in the temporary room was what I'd taken with me, but it was too much to juggle. I handed Tex my garment bag of cocktail attire instead. His forehead furrowed.

"Play the role of dutiful husband just once. It'll help sell your cover."

He took the bag. "This job can't end fast enough." He grinned to let me know he was kidding.

We followed the signs to the upper deck and, eventually, to a private staircase. There was a sign outside that said the Sanctuary.

Lenny was waiting for us in the hallway. "It's about time," he said. He seemed nervous. "Which one of you has my passkey?"

"I do." I reluctantly handed over our ticket to snoop. I hadn't opened nearly enough doors to part with it just yet.

Lenny slipped the card into the breast pocket of his

uniform then pulled two black key cards out of his pants pocket. "These are for you. A porter will bring your luggage soon. There's fruit and pastries on the table from this morning, and bottles of water in the fridge. Someone will come by with a fresh tray tomorrow morning."

"That isn't necessary."

"You're the talent, right? That's part of your contract."

"That's right," Tex said. "If I remember correctly, you made a specific request for Lone Star Beer."

"Not tonight," Lenny said. "Beer has to be purchased at the bar by the pool. There's water, soda, and juice inside the fridge in your room. The captain sent you a complimentary bottle of wine. If you don't need anything else, I have to go put out a fire by the photo booth."

"We're fine," Tex said, and I added, "Who else knew we were in room three-oh-seven?"

Lenny looked back and forth between our faces. I glanced at Tex, but his expressionless cop face was in place.

"Nobody. Why?"

"There was a phone call."

"That was probably a member of the crew. We usually leave three-oh-seven open for the crew to use. That's how I knew it wasn't occupied."

"But—"

Tex cut me off. "Thanks, Lenny."

Lenny shook Tex's outstretched hand. He nodded and left.

It seemed prudent to enter the room before anything else, so I held the key card in front of the lock, and the mechanism clicked. The door popped open, and we went inside.

Thoughts of what we'd just learned left my mind as I took in our new quarters.

Tex whistled.

Compared to our first room, a closet, and our second room, which was more modest, the luxury suite was palatial. A dining room table that sat twelve was nestled in a kitchen complete with microwave, toaster, coffee maker, and panini press. Past that was a sitting room with a TV and entertainment console. A baby grand piano was in the far corner.

A baby grand piano!

Directly ahead of us was a view of the ocean—or there would be the next morning when the sun was up. Tonight, floor-length curtains revealed the deep, purply-black night sky and mysterious dark-blue waters. They were touched by glimmers of light reflected from the exterior illumination on the boat. The view wrapped around our room to the right, where a hot tub that would accommodate Kate plus Eight gently bubbled.

I turned to Tex. "Where's the bed?"

"Who needs a bed? We've got a hot tub."

"I plan to take advantage of the view and the hot tub, too, but the talent requires eight hours of sleep."

"We'll sleep when we're dead."

"If we don't figure out what's happening on this cruise, that may come sooner rather than later."

I left Tex staring out at the ocean and carried my garment bag toward the bedroom. It was a sizeable suite, complete with another view of the ocean, a balcony, and a couple of towels folded in the shape of swans in the center of the king-sized bed, deterring me from lying down for a rest.

I hung my garment bag in the closet. Tex stood over the open drawer of his nightstand and emptied his pockets.

I was thrilled to have finally settled into our room. While Tex explored the rest of the room, I set my cosmetics up on the bathroom vanity. My collection of Apple Polish lipstick came from the estate of Judy Johnson. She was a popcorn girl at the Casa Linda theater in North Dallas. She kept a file pay stubs that indicated she made twenty cents an hour more than the ushers—a thirty percent difference at the time—along with a couple of flirty notes from the ushers bemoaning that fact. Among her treasure trove of lipsticks were several unopened tubes of Cherries in the Snow and Fire and Ice, but like Doris Day, I favored the coral-pink hue of Apple Polish. I was still waiting for someone to make a reasonable replacement.

When I came out of the bathroom, Tex stood by the sliding doors with his back to me. His broad shoulders were set off by the darkness of the sea in front of him. The breeze tossed his hair around his head. He had his hands in the pockets of his trousers, and I couldn't help myself. I snuck up and threaded my arms through his and hugged him from behind. He was taller than I was, but I could still peek over his shoulder at the vastness of the sea as we cut through the water. Overhead, a near-full moon provided a pan of light that winked off of the water. I turned my head to the side and laid it against Tex's shoulder. It was a rare moment of peace within the storm of our lives.

Tex turned around and kissed me. His hands went into my hair, and he backed me away from the sliding doors.

Turns out the towel animals on the bedspread weren't much of a deterrent after all.

Afterward, we reconvened at the dining room table. In

the absence of beer, Tex uncorked the bottle of chardonnay and poured two glasses. He handed me one, and we sat across from each other at the table, two halves of a civilized married couple enjoying a complimentary glass of wine in our bougie cabin.

"There is a very good chance we've already interacted with the burglar," Tex said after taking a sip of wine.

"You do have a one-track mind, don't you?"

He grinned. "Now that my mind is clear, I can focus on the case."

"I do not want to think about how you solved all of those cases back in Dallas before we met."

"If it's any consolation, my closure rate went up after I met you."

"Somehow, I doubt I had anything to do with that, but I appreciate the attempt to make me feel special." I took a sip of my wine and closed my eyes, appreciating the subtle buttery nuance of the wine as it coated my tongue and slid down my throat. "Back to our current dilemma. What would you like to do next?"

"It's not what I should do next. It's you."

"I'll bite. What should I do next?"

"You should have an affair."

CHAPTER THIRTEEN

Not for nothing, Tex's suggestion made sense.

I found a certain measure of freedom in pretending to be married to Tex. Our covers created two distinct personas: me, the entertaining diva, expected to literally take center stage, and Tex, my manager husband, who was expected to do little more than collect payment. I didn't know how much Tex knew about Doris Day's manager-husband and his business activities in regard to her career, but I sincerely hoped Tex would not use him as a template.

Tex's suggestion that I have an affair worked on a number of levels. Persephone, the decorator, already suspected me of cheating on Tex, and Meg and Mavis Stork seemed to want me to start something with the reclusive cosmonaut staying in the unoccupied wing. My roaming those levels I had no business roaming could easily fall under the umbrella of infidelity. It helped that the Stork sisters encouraged the hubba-hubba aspect of my meeting with the cosmonaut. I doubted they would rat me out to my spouse.

I finished my wine and stood. "What time is it?"

Tex checked his wrist out of habit, but his wrist was bare, so the effort was futile.

"Where's your watch?"

"Didn't bring one," he said. "We're on a cruise. It's supposed to be relaxing. I didn't plan on watching the clock."

"We're on a cruise, but this isn't a vacation. I'm on the clock. Shouldn't my manager be able to keep me on schedule?"

"You're supposed to have your people to keep you on schedule."

"You're part of 'my people.' I don't want to be insensitive, but my other 'people' is dead." I ran that sentence back through my mind. "Homer. He was my only contact on the ship. He was the one who should have kept me on schedule, and now he can't."

"Somebody's going to have to step up and take over his responsibilities. The ship needs a purser." While I mulled over what that meant to me as the hired help, Tex pulled his bat phone out of his pocket and tapped the screen. "To answer your question, it's midnight."

"Is that early or late?"

"Your guess is as good as mine. I'm guessing people either turned in early or are on the mezzanine with the band."

"I slept in this morning, so my clock is wonky. I'm taking my chances for a clear coast."

"Which way are you heading?"

"I don't know. Do you have any suggestions?"

Tex opened a folio and pulled out our itinerary. It was typed on a sheet of Big Bro Security letterhead. He flipped it over and drew an *X* on the page. "We're here." He tapped the *X* a few times, leaving small dots on the paper. "If you go this way"—he drew a line to the right of the *X*—"you'll reach a set of stairs that will get you one flight up or one flight down." He drew diagonal lines up and down coming off the first line and drew a circle next to the top line. "Up goes to the pool. That's a popular destination, and nobody will question you going there. The Tossed Pebbles are playing tonight, and anybody who isn't sitting out their first night on the boat is probably there. If you do go that direction, you won't avoid being seen. That can work in your favor. If you think you're in a tight spot, get to where you're surrounded by people."

"What about the other direction?"

Tex stared at the paper. He drew a wave with a flat line over it. "The stairs will take you down to the ocean-viewing level."

"The glass bottom," I said, remembering something from our initial briefing.

"Yes. I doubt anybody will be there tonight." He drew a greater-than symbol above the line indicating the direction in which to head. His scrawled map looked a junior high school student's algebra homework. "If you cross the glass bottom, you'll end up at another exit that will take you up to the lido deck—"

"Where I found Homer's body."

"Right. Once you're on the lido deck, you know how to get to the opposite side of the ship and to the other levels."

He studied his drawing for a few seconds then looked up and held the piece of paper out to me. "You want this?"

I tapped my temple. "I think I've got it. Up is the pool and the crowd, down is aquatic life and mermaids."

"You think there's more than one mermaid?"

"The number of mermaids on this cruise is at the bottom of my list of things to figure out."

Tex folded the paper on top of itself and carried it to the

trash bin. He seemed to think twice about throwing it away, and I understood why. If the wrong person got ahold of anything that indicated Tex and I were not who we seemed, it would put our cover stories at risk and put us both in danger. No matter which crime we planned to expose, it was not the time to forget there was a murderer on board.

I left the Sanctuary. I'd been hoping to pass a porter with a luggage cart stacked high with vintage turquoise Samsonite luggage, but the hallways were both empty and quiet. It was a good thing I'd retrieved my garment bag and train case; it looked as if the Templetons would be luggage-less until tomorrow morning.

Being alone on the ship gave me the unique opportunity to study the rest of its design concept. Homer had said the *New Nautilus* was an old ship that had recently been renovated to fit the nostalgic theme, which would have been a fantastic job for me at Mad for Mod. Sadly, Persephone had not only missed the bull's-eye, she'd missed the whole dartboard.

In a conversation with Tex years ago, I'd likened decorating to detecting. I explained how I worked, sometimes starting with a client's favorite item and building an entire concept around it. When a client didn't know what they wanted, we walked through my showroom or, in a few cases, my inventory. Their response to one or two details could inform the direction of an entire room, and a jumping-off point was all I needed. The challenge of decorating a cruise ship in a mid-sixties theme would have made me salivate not to mention given me a chance to use a lot of fixtures that currently sat in storage. I would have bid on the gig if I'd known about it, but Galveston was far enough away from Dallas not to have made it onto my radar.

As I walked through the hallway, my decorator's eye found missed opportunities left, right, and center. The first thing I would do was tear out the carpet. Dark-blue industrial-grade might be practical, but nothing about a sixties-theme cruise ship should be practical. I had a virtual Rolodex filled with suppliers, some of whom still produced patterns from seventy years ago.

Most people associated carpeting with the seventies, when the industry exploded, but by 1951, there was already about six million square yards of carpeting in homes across America. And while shag did hit its stride in the late sixties, as I tried to imagine fluffy carpeting in the hallways of a cruise ship, I instantly discarded the nostalgic choice. Too messy, too much upkeep.

Other options existed, of course. Shaw still produced some of the more classic patterns that worked in mid-century modern rooms. Avedon, a small-scale diamond, would certainly be tasteful, but who expected cruises to be tasteful? The boat should be fun with a capital *F*.

A carpet in aqua, with boomerang shapes of darker blue and perhaps yellow, would light up the hallway. No—switch that up. Yellow carpet with blue pattern—less expected—would make anyone stepping foot onto the boat feel as if they'd stepped into a time warp. If given a high-speed-internet pass and half an hour, I could find someone who'd reproduced a mermaid-themed wallpaper that would work.

My mind played with the lines of the hallway, imagining retro shower decals that looked like etched glass for the rooms, coordinating fabrics used for curtains, bedspreads, and upholstery, and quirky touches in each of the guest rooms to tie them all together. It was almost a sin that the cruise didn't have a tiki lounge. I would have had a field day with that!

As I continued through the hallway, I couldn't help wondering if the lackluster design choices belonged to Persephone or the owner of the boat. They already seemed to understand the novelty of having mermaid sightings on their trip, so incorporating other fun elements was a no-brainer.

Even if the designer hadn't wanted to rely on kitsch to bring the mid-century theme to life, they could have taken a page out of the playbook of the TWA Hotel in New York. The once-busy airport terminal now stood like a jewel in the middle of Queens, retrofitted with tulip tables and bubble lamps, retro travel posters on the walls of the guest rooms to play up the nostalgic theme. The cruise could have done all that the hotel did and more, becoming a floating time capsule and paying tribute to an entire canon of cruise-themed history.

But it didn't.

I recalled that Tex's instructions were to go up or down depending on the circumstances. As I contemplated which direction to take, something moved at the end of the hall. The sudden motion surprised me. I proceeded carefully, motivated by a combination of curiosity and apprehension. I reached a door at the end of the hallway. Someone was on the other side.

CHAPTER FOURTEEN

THE DOOR OPENED ONTO A CARPETED LANDING, AND THE culprit came into sight: a Roomba.

The flat, circular vacuum headed toward a wall then changed direction as it got close. It headed for my feet. I stayed rooted in place. The Roomba changed direction again and moved toward the wall.

Just because I used authentic materials and original items in my room designs didn't mean I was opposed to technology that would make my life easier, and something about the small, roving vacuum cleaner reminded me of the novelty of atomic design. One of my closest friends had started as a client, and I'd designed for her and her then-husband a kitchen inspired by the one in *The Glass Bottom Boat*. I'd even had my handyman at the time retrofit a Roomba into a boxy cage fabricated out of flashing and painted to look exactly like the one that gave Doris Day so much trouble in the movie. She told me it was popular at dinner parties.

I picked up the device and ran my fingers around the

perimeter of it until I found the off switch. The motor went silent. I set it down. As I straightened, I heard footsteps below me, followed by a female voice calling up.

"Hello? Is someone there?" Footsteps sounded on the staircase in front of me. Before I had time to flee, a deeply tanned blonde with freckles rounded the corner. "I thought I heard someone. You're the singer, right?"

"Yes." I had a strong sensation that I'd met the woman before, but I didn't know where. She looked friendly enough, but I'd learned from experience that freckles and fluffy blond hair could help sell that appearance.

"Are you okay?" she asked.

Her voice was familiar, too, and after a stretched-out moment, it clicked. "You're the mermaid?" It started as a statement but ended as a question.

She held up both hands. "Guilty as charged. Most people don't recognize me when I'm on the boat. What gave me away?"

Instead of answering, I stared at her head. When she was in the water, she was a redhead, but that night, her hair was blond and cropped to chin length. I must have stared a little longer than was polite because she put her hand on her head. "Is my wig crooked? I didn't look in the mirror before leaving my lab."

"It's fine," I said. "But you were a redhead earlier."

Jennifer grinned. "It's all part of the mermaid act. It's easier to wear a wig when I'm dry than when I'm in the water, so I go *au naturel* when I wear the tail, and I wear the wig when I'm on the boat. Most people aren't as observant as you."

I pointed at the patch on her vest that read JENNIFER, NEW NAUTILUS DIVE TEAM. "It wasn't your wig that gave you away, it was your vest. Lenny told us the mermaid was also the dive instructor."

Jennifer put her hand over the patch. "I'll have to talk to Lenny about that. He's not supposed to give away my secret."

I couldn't tell her that at the time, Lenny had been more concerned with the dead body Tex and I had just called him about and might not have been thinking clearly, so I said nothing.

"Are you lost?" she asked.

"Not exactly. I'm out for a late-night walk. I heard a noise at the end of the hall and came in here to investigate."

"You heard me?"

"I heard a Roomba."

She shook her head. "The ship doesn't use Roombas anymore."

I stepped backward, revealing the inactive device. Jennifer's face went pale. She stared at the device for a few seconds then looked at me as if checking to see whether I thought her reaction was odd. It was, but I didn't want her to know I thought so. She scooped up the device and flipped it over. "I turned it off," I said, assuming that was what puzzled her.

"What?" she said, but before I repeated myself, she added, "Oh, right. Lenny must have missed this one." She tucked it under her arm and sandwiched it between her elbow and her torso. "They used to run them while the ship was docked, but that policy changed after—" She bit her lip as if deciding whether she should finish her sentence.

I remembered something Tex had once told me about interrogation. Sometimes, it wasn't a question that got the information. It was an awkward silence.

Tex's strategy worked.

"There was an accident once when a Roomba surprised a woman on the lido deck. She lost her balance and fell overboard."

I didn't expect that!

"Was she—she didn't—what happened?"

"The ship anchored, and she was pulled in to safety. The whole incident put the ship behind schedule, and they didn't reach Cozumel until four hours later than expected."

"They?"

Jennifer shrugged. "It happened before I was hired. Technically, it's the reason I was hired. The cruise didn't have a dedicated dive team to rescue her."

"Isn't the crew trained in safety protocols?" I asked, not solely for investigative purposes. A passenger on a cruise ship did like to know there was someone ready to handle an emergency.

"Yes. The whole crew has STCW certification. That's Standards of Training, Certification, and Watchkeeping for Seafarers. It's a US regulation for anybody working a seagoing ship. People can apply for jobs and get the training after, but applicants with certification get prioritized."

"Then it shouldn't have been a big deal."

"Trust me. When a passenger falls off a cruise ship, it's a big deal. It doesn't matter how efficiently someone steps in to rescue her."

"Was she okay?"

"She was livid. She threatened to sue, but the company found a way to appease her."

"All because of a robotic vacuum? That seems a little extreme." And a little clumsy on the part of the passenger, but I didn't share that last bit.

"Not if you remember where we are. Activities are to be

monitored, and there's supposed to be someone around to oversee the safety of the passengers." She waved the robotic vacuum at me. "These guys represent a real threat once we leave the dock. They operate on sensors, so you never know when they're going to change direction. Besides, there are no carpets on the lido deck, so there were a lot of questions about negligence and why it was there in the first place."

"Did the captain ever find out who was responsible?"

"It was no secret. You must have met Homer. He was the boatswain back then, and he had his fingers in everything. If he hadn't jumped in to save her, he probably would have lost his job."

"He's not the boatswain anymore, though."

"We were all shocked when the cruise company gave him a promotion. A lot of people weren't happy about that."

Not knowing the hierarchy of positions on a boat, I didn't know who ranked above whom, but Jennifer had just eliminated any questions I had about Homer's new job title. I couldn't tell if Jennifer was trying to plant a story about him or if she was just naturally chatty, but the longer we stood in the stairwell, the more I wondered about everything Tex and I thought we knew about that cruise.

It wasn't long before Jennifer circled back to her original question. "What are you doing in this part of the ship?"

"I wanted a chance to explore, and I thought this hallway would be quiet."

"You mean you didn't expect to run into a workaholic." She gave me a sheepish smile. "I'm not just a mermaid. I'm an aquatic biologist."

"Is there much of a need for that on a cruise?"

Her face fell. "No. There should be, but nobody cares about the unique aquatic life we pass through on our trip. I applied for the job as dive instructor because the *New Nautilus* has a glass bottom, and that means I can study the fish in my spare time. I didn't know until I accepted their offer that part of the job was dressing up like a mermaid to entertain the passengers."

"From what I saw the other day, you accepted that responsibility gracefully."

Jennifer smiled. "The first time, I admit, I had a chip on my shoulder. To take my entire education and subjugate it into an overly sexualized role straight out of a Disney movie was not what I signed up for. But then I saw people's reactions to seeing me in the water. And when I mingled with the passengers, they lit up. It wasn't just the children on the cruise but the adults too. Sheer delight. I leaned into it. I found a way to get people interested in what goes on in the water. Sign-ups for the diving excursions went up. It just goes to show, sometimes the opportunities we need are already there. They just don't look like we expect."

"That's a nice way to look at it."

"What can I say?" She shrugged. "When you spend hours a day as a mermaid, you learn to go with the flow."

Crisis averted, I recognized that I was in a restricted part of the boat after hours. It would be very easy for someone to see my behavior as suspicious. While I was turning a cover story over in my mind, Jennifer asked, "Will you keep my secret?"

"What secret?"

"That I'm not really a mermaid."

"Deal."

We parted ways. Jennifer headed to the underbelly of the boat while I reentered the hallway.

I didn't know what time it was, but it had to be after

midnight. Despite my pre-cruise efforts to reset my internal body clock, the excitement of the day had left me tired. I didn't relish returning to the Sanctuary empty-handed, so to speak, and I felt as if I'd blown an opportunity to discover information that might help Tex and me in our investigation. Then again, I wasn't completely empty-handed: I'd learned about Homer's former role as the boatswain, his surprise promotion, and the legal battles that the *New Nautilus* had after a Roomba sent a guest overboard.

Come to think of it, that was an awful lot of information for a brief interlude with a mermaid.

CHAPTER FIFTEEN

As I headed down the hallway, faint strains of music played from somewhere else on the boat, accompanied by laughter, occasionally interrupted by a voice over a loudspeaker. The party by the pool sounded as if it was still going strong. Aside from Jennifer, there were no signs of any other people wandering the ship.

When I'd first left our new room, I told Tex I was taking a walk, and that became a convenient cover for scoping out the ship. But there was another reason I'd wanted to scope out the ship, and it had nothing to do with getting answers for Nasty.

It had to do with fear.

Years of singing along to Doris Day albums had helped train my voice in the same way Doris Day herself had trained hers by singing along with Ella Fitzgerald recordings in her formative years. I didn't doubt that I knew the lyrics to Doris Day's songbook, but my singing usually took place in my studio, surrounded by an audience of furniture with right angles. When Rocky was present, he liked to join in, tipping his head back and howling like a werewolf at a full moon. It made for an entertaining duet, but I doubted it was what the paying patrons on the cruise ship wanted.

I located the Nautilus Shell, where I was expected to perform. The door was closed, but I could see into the room through a small round window. Maybe I just needed some time inside, time to get familiar with my surroundings, to stand on the stage and imagine what it would be like to face a room filled with guests there to hear me sing. Or maybe I needed to feign a case of food poisoning, pretend I was too sick to fulfill my duties, and be done with the whole thing. Nobody said I would get a medal for making a fool of myself.

Earlier, when I'd first spoken to Persephone, she said she was behind schedule in getting the room ready, but from the looks of things, she was more than just behind. It looked as if Persephone had gotten frustrated in the process of decorating and walked off mid-job.

Voices grew closer. I pushed against the door, and it gave under my weight. Once inside, I closed it behind me. I tried to move away, but the fabric of my skirt had gotten caught. I quickly reopened the door and pulled the fabric inside then shut it again.

If the people in the hallway saw me, they would no doubt investigate—unless they were too absorbed in their activities to have spotted me. I stood as still as I could and waited for the voices to pass.

Unfortunately, the voices didn't pass.

They stopped outside the nightclub. The door handle to the room jiggled, but it didn't open. I held my breath. Why had the door opened under my hand but not theirs?

"Locked," a male voice said.

"I have the key," a female voice replied. It was Persephone, the one person who had a reason to come to the nightclub, considering how much work she still had to do to get it ready for tomorrow. Explaining my presence, in the dark, was going to be problematic—even if I did offer my considerable decorating skills and volunteer once again to pitch in.

There was nothing inside the nightclub to hide me. A slight dance floor sat at the base of the stage, and the space for the tables was empty while the decorating was underway. It was just a matter of time until the door opened and I was found, unless—

I didn't stop to think about whether I would be seen. I ran behind the stage. A flashlight—still on—sat on a chair, and a thin beam of light cast a glow over the various surfaces. I peeked around the side of the stage and watched the door. Persephone's head was visible through the round window in the door.

Coming off my conversation with Jennifer, I had Homer on the brain, and I recalled the way Persephone had spoken about him. I didn't know a lot about Persephone, but one thing I'd picked up on when we spoke earlier was how she had talked about Homer. I got the feeling the two of them had been involved in some manner, appropriate or not, and that she had been the jilted lover. She wouldn't be the first woman to stab her ex in a fit of rage, and the knife used to stab him could easily have been among the equipment she used in her job as decorator or taken from the kitchen attached to the Nautilus Shell. But if she *had* stabbed him, would she be that quick to bounce back with another member of the crew? Or was it possible she hadn't acted alone?

The door handle rattled again. The lock held. I lowered

myself onto a chair and strained to hear something that would let me know if I had company.

Persephone cursed. Her voice was still far away, distorted by the barrier of the door. "Let's go back to my room. After tomorrow night, nobody's going to come see the impersonator anyway."

I crept closer to the door, still hidden by the stage, and peeked around the corner. Persephone was with someone. A man. I hoped to catch a glimpse of him, something to refer to later, but the same barrier that kept them from seeing me kept me from seeing them.

The shadow of feet under the door receded. I waited several seconds before reentering the room. When it seemed safe, I came out front and scanned the room. The whole reason I was there was to get comfortable, but my nervous system was lit up like a Christmas tree.

I crept to the door and opened it. The hallway was empty. Persephone and her companion weren't there, but something else was: a piece of paper. I picked it up, hoping it was a clue to the man's identity.

And it was, just not the clue I'd expected. It was the handwritten map Tex had made of the boat when we were back in our room.

I stared at the torn piece of paper for longer than I needed to. I'd been right there when Tex made the sketch, the glass bottom and the lido deck, the diagonal lines that pointed up and down, the circle that designated our room. He'd asked me if I wanted to take it with me, and I'd declined. This piece of paper should have been back in our room, in the trash, or in his pocket, but not here, not in the hallway, not unless Tex himself had been the person who dropped it.

That thought expanded in my mind like an eyedropper of dye in a glass of water, blooming into a cloud that overtook the rest of the contents. I had no doubt that Persephone had been the woman with the key. Her presence made sense. But until I discovered Tex's map, my thoughts had leaned toward Homer having rejected her, and her possibly having an accomplice in his murder.

My mind reached for new threads to connect, a pattern I hadn't seen before. I came up blank. Tex had met Persephone mere minutes after I'd met her, when I pretended to be on the phone with him and he showed up in person. He had introduced himself as my husband, and both Tex and I interpreted her response the same way: as if she thought I was having an affair.

So what was *she* doing with my fake husband now?

And equally troubling: Why had she invited him back to her room?

CHAPTER SIXTEEN

Nasty sent us on this mission with one guideline: Discover who was stealing from guests on the cruise ship. The job was predicated on one fact: Someone was not who they seemed. That detail was easy to believe when I applied it to the guests and the crew, but Tex? The last person I expected to keep secrets from me was my fake husband.

I folded the slip of paper with Tex's rudimentary map and tucked it into the patch pocket of my yellow dress. There had to be an explanation. There *had* to be. Despite Tex's past reputation as a toxic bachelor, I didn't believe the man I knew had been fabricated out of thin air. There might have been a time when he would have seized an opportunity while going undercover, but that ship had sailed.

My nerves were shattered, and I no longer cared about spending time in the nightclub. With any luck, the guests would have such a fun time with the band tonight that they would forget all about the Doris Day impersonator on the boat. Meg and Mavis Stork might be eager to hear my rendition of "Bright and Shiny," but they were already on my side. I didn't see them dissing me if I hit a wrong note.

I headed to the Sanctuary. A part of me still believed I would find Tex with his feet up on the coffee table, watching whatever sporting event he could find on TV. I scanned my key card and gained entry then called out, "Honey? I'm home."

There was no reply.

If we had still been in our original room, a glance around the interior would have let me know if Tex was there, but in the spacious luxury suite, confirming I was alone required a little more effort. I walked past the dining room table and looked around the living room then doubled back and checked the bathroom and bedroom. The sliding doors to the balcony were open, but the room was empty. Tex wasn't here.

I had enough to worry about. Tex's loyalty wasn't going on that list.

* * *

THE NEXT MORNING, I woke with Tex's arm slung across my torso. The curtains were open, and bright sunlight flooded the room. I turned toward the clock. It was five thirty.

At home, this was the time I regularly woke. In the summer, I swam laps at Crestwood, and in the winter at the Gaston Swim Club. Both pools opened at six, so five thirty gave me just enough time to throw on a suit and a coverup and head out, experiencing Dallas before the rest of the world joined the rat race. On trash days, I sometimes even went home with pieces of furniture that had been left by the curb, items that needed a little TLC to come back to life. As an independent businesswoman, I was a big fan of one-hundred-percent-off inventory.

I should have been tired, but my body hadn't gotten the memo. Even though the cruise was a vacation and I was pretending to be someone other than myself, there was no reason I couldn't keep up with my schedule while here. I turned away from Tex and threw off the covers. His arm pulled me back toward him, and he nuzzled his face into my shoulder. We'd woken like this many times before, but today was different.

"Mmmmmmmmm," Tex said. It turned into something between a snore and a hum. "Don't get up yet."

With a little effort, I rolled over and faced him.

Tex shifted his arm. "How'd you make out last night?"

"Not as well as you, it seems."

"What do you mean?" Tex was suddenly more awake. He propped himself up on his elbow. "Didn't you get my note?"

"What note?"

"The one I left in the hallway outside the nightclub."

"You admit to being there? In the hallway? With Persephone?"

"Why wouldn't I admit to it? I figure you heard me from inside the club."

"Hold up." I propped on my elbow, mirroring Tex. "How did you know I was in the nightclub?"

"How many people on this ship dress like you?"

"You saw me?"

"I did, but the decorator didn't."

"How's that possible?"

"I might have distracted her."

"I knew it!"

I threw the covers back and stood. Sometime last night,

after returning to the empty room, I'd changed into a pair of pink satin pajamas from the estate of Tatiana Novas. Tatiana was the administrative assistant at Bristol Jarvis, an airplane parts manufacturer who at one time offered women a distinct career path. Tatiana wasn't the first former employee of the company that I'd gotten to know after acquiring her estate, but she may have been among the most notorious. Not only did she keep a room filled with airplane manufacturers in line, but her eagle eye had caught a typo on a supply form and saved the company $1.4 million dollars. The company was quick to reward her with free travel for life, expanding her worldview from the greater Dallas area to include Japan, Europe, and Egypt. Her estate had been expertly catalogued, often including one-page stories about where she'd purchased the souvenirs she brought home. She'd had a real taste for Chinese silk pajamas with frog closures, buying them in bulk and leaving several sets still in their packaging.

I wasn't sure what Tex wore on the bottom half of his body, but his chest was bare. He didn't move. As I stood in front of the sliding doors, I narrowed my eyes. Tex didn't look guilty of anything. In fact, he looked amused.

"What do you think you know?"

"You were with Persephone."

"I was," he said.

"And Persephone invited you back to her room."

"She did."

"And you went?"

"I did."

"I see." And I did. I saw that Tex had spotted an opportunity to find out more about Persephone, and he had taken it. His boyish charm, coupled with Persephone's conclusion that I was cheating on him, thus leaving him the jilted, available man on the cruise ship, would have paved that road. Tex sent me off in one of two directions: up to the pool or down to the glass bottom. Based on our plan, he never would have expected me to be in the nightclub, but when he discovered me there, he protected my cover.

I thought back on what had transpired while I was on one side of the nightclub door and Persephone and Tex were on the other. "The door to the nightclub wasn't locked, was it?"

Instead of answering, Tex rolled over and picked up a small black cube from his bedside table. He held it between his thumb and forefinger. It was about two inches wide. He extended his arm and held out the cube, and I took it.

"What is this?"

"A magnet. I brought one for you too. It temporarily renders the magnetic strip on the key cards inactive. When I saw fabric from your dress sticking out from the door of the nightclub, I thought something had happened to you. Then the door opened and the fabric disappeared, and I realized you were behind that door. Seemed like a good idea to keep Persephone from finding that out."

I turned my back to Tex and sat on the edge of the bed. Outside past our balcony, the sun was bright, and the sky was clear. From where I sat, I could see a broad stretch of blue-green ocean dotted with spots of sunlight reflected off the surface. Tiny crests of white foam tipped peaks of water. The cruise ship sliced through them, barely rocking as it advanced toward Mexico. Crisp, salty air filled my lungs. It was a marvel of Mother Nature, tranquility in a world otherwise filled with disturbances. Stare at the ocean long enough and you'll believe life was serene.

"For a moment, I thought you and Persephone..." My voice trailed off.

Tex pretended to be insulted. "A little faith, please. Besides, you're the one having an affair."

"Am I?"

"Persephone thinks so. She spent a fair amount of time telling me I could do better."

At that, I spun to face him. "She said that?"

"Oh, she said that and more. Persephone isn't going to be named the head of your fan club anytime soon."

"What else did she say?"

"That you're not qualified to perform on this ship. That you're a fraud. That she doesn't know how you got the job, but after tonight, it won't be a problem anymore."

I scooted onto the bed and backed up against the headboard. I stretched my legs out in front of me. I still wasn't over the novelty of being able to bend my previously injured knee, so I reached down and grabbed my ankles. I pulled my feet toward me and sat with my soles pressed against each other and my knees sticking out. I set the blocky magnet on my left knee, and it tumbled off and landed on the bedspread. Tex picked it up and balanced it on my knee again, and this time, it remained in place.

I stared at the magnet and answered Tex's question. "I'm scheduled to sing tonight. Persephone thinks I'm going to out myself as a fraud." I picked up the magnet and squeezed. The sharp edges bit into my hand. "She's not wrong."

"I thought you were going to sing along with a recording?"

"That was the plan, but what if the equipment doesn't work? Homer was supposed to make sure everything went smoothly, but with Homer dead, we're up the ocean without a paddle."

"Do you want to back out of it?"

Tex knew how much was riding on my performance. It was the one detail that had gotten us preferential treatment and allowed us to get away with demands that regular guests could not. My role as the entertainment had raised our profile more than if we'd pretended to be winners of a contest. But Tex's question wasn't about protecting our identity. It was about me. My fear. I'd watched Tex go undercover while investigating a crime more than once, and I knew it was the most effective way to find out information. If I canceled, he would find another way to get what we needed, but was that what I wanted? To be the weak link in our partnership?

"No," I said. "I don't want to cancel. You can count on me to do my part."

"Good. I'll do what I can to make sure you're singing to a sympathetic crowd."

That should have made me feel better. I didn't tell Tex it did not.

CHAPTER SEVENTEEN

MY PLAN TO GET UP AND GO SWIMMING BEFORE THE REST OF the boat woke up was off the table. Tex and I dozed a little longer, then I got up, showered, and dressed in a short-sleeved white turtleneck trimmed with yellow and a matching yellow skort from the estate of Elizabeth Hollier. Elizabeth had been the wife of the manager of the Preston Hollow Golf Course just north of Dallas, and her wardrobe indicated her love of the game. This wasn't the first collection of golf attire I'd acquired but it was the most well organized. When I first came into possession of Elizabeth's estate, I'd found twenty-seven one-gallon Ziploc bags, each holding a coordinated golfing ensemble. She had cropped pants and Bermuda shorts and polo shirts in colors that had since been discontinued by Crayola. Judging from the wear pattern on the socks, she seemed to have favored the pink, blue, and purple shades. The yellow was in near-mint condition.

Instead of pulling on the yellow-and-white argyle socks Elizabeth might have favored, I slipped my bare feet into yellow Keds. Until our luggage was delivered to our newest room, I was working with a limited wardrobe.

I left Tex in the bedroom and went to investigate the coffee situation. At home, I used either a Mr. Coffee or an electric coffeepot from the late sixties, but neither was available. A Nespresso machine sat on the counter next to a basket of individual coffee pods. It wasn't the environmentalist's choice, but it would have to do.

After prepping a cup of coffee, I sliced a cantaloupe and sat down to eat. Tex had started a case file of notations about our first day on the ship, now strewn across the table. I scanned them while I let my coffee cool.

The last time I had gotten to see Tex's investigative process up close and personal was when a serial killer had terrorized Dallas. Tex's connection to the case landed him a suspension. He commandeered a camper and ran a one-man investigation from the corner of a public parking lot, fueled in large part by Chinese food. Until that case, I had thought of Tex as a cop first and a person second. After that, I knew there was no way to split the two. Tex was a package deal. It took me a long time to realize that in that regard, he was just like me.

The notes on the table were exhaustive. There were several pages, each listing a person we had met and any possible suspicious behavior. Lenny, Willow, Persephone, Jennifer, and Meg and Mavis Stork were all there. So was Captain Vladimir Komarov.

Tex joined me in the living room. He reached down and snatched a slice of cantaloupe from my plate. "See anything I missed?"

I picked up the page for the cosmonaut. "This is you."

"Nobody else knows that."

"But nobody else is going to look at these notes."

"We don't know that." He crossed the room and inserted a pod into the Nespresso, positioned a mug beneath it, then turned and leaned against the counter while the coffee brewed. He wore the same shirt and suit trousers he'd worn yesterday, both of which were in need of a refresh. His arms were tan with a white stripe where his watch had been. He crossed his arms, and his biceps flexed.

"You never told me what you learned last night," he said.

I set the page with Komarov's name on the table and slid out the page with Jennifer's name. Until last night, the only thing we'd known about her was that she was the resident mermaid and dive instructor.

"I ran into Jennifer. Playing the resident mermaid isn't her favorite part of the job."

"She said that?"

"She said a lot of things. She's an aquatic biologist. She seems to care about the scientific aspect of her job. She said initially, she saw playing the mermaid as a sexualized fantasy, but it ended up being what got people's attention. She started booking more dive excursions, and she had more visitors to the glass bottom."

"Did you see it?"

"The glass bottom? No."

"Where did this conversation take place?"

"In the stairwell. I heard a noise, and I went to check it out. Jennifer heard me and came up the stairs to find out what was causing all the commotion."

"What was it?"

"A Roomba." I summarized what I'd learned from Jennifer last night: the woman who fell overboard, the safety certifications of every member of the ship, the heroics of

Homer, who had also been negligent in collecting the Roombas in the first place, and the promotion that came out of it all. "I don't know if I believe her, though. When she saw the Roomba, she got this look on her face—like she'd seen a ghost."

Tex's coffee finished brewing. He carried his mug to the table and sat across from me. Steam rose from the surface of the mug, and the scent of bitter coffee dissipated through the room.

"Write that down."

"Which part?"

"All of it. Right now, we're collecting impressions. We don't know what's important. As we discover details, they'll reveal a pattern. They'll tell a story that will lead us to the thief. Most of our details won't fit, but some will emerge that do."

I studied Tex and replayed my conversation with Jennifer in my mind. It had sounded so innocent at the time. The dive instructor working in the science lab. That was exactly where I would have expected her to be. The explanation about being the mermaid? That too. But she was outside the boat at the exact time Tex and I found Homer's body, and that might not have been coincidence. There were very few alibis as solid as being in a mermaid suit in the ocean when a body was discovered, but it would take only a little planning to be able to pull that off.

"Jennifer said the woman who fell was livid. She threatened to sue the company. But the interesting thing is that the company didn't fire Homer. They promoted him."

"There's a common business practice that promotes people to a position where they're ineffectual. It's an easy way to deal with a problem."

"You would think a company would want good employees working for them."

"Homer's not around to tell us his side of the story, but that might have been an isolated incident. He might have been employee of the year before that accident."

I interrupted Tex. "Do we know if he was?" Tex's face clouded. "Do we know anything about Homer except for the fact that he was our contact? *Why* was he our contact? What did Nasty tell you about him? Why did she trust him? Is it a coincidence that the only cruise employee who knows why we're here is dead? Do we need to worry about that? I, for one, would like to know a little bit more about this job before we proceed."

Tex stood. He went to the kitchen and opened a cabinet filled with processed snacks. Bright-blue-and-yellow packages of cookies were waiting for us whenever the craving hit. Neither Tex nor I ate a lot of junk food, so I figured the cookies would still be there when our trip was over.

Tex reached behind the cookies and pulled out a folder. It was white, the same color as the interior of the cabinet. He carried it to the table and placed it in front of me.

"What's this?"

"Open it."

I opened the folder. Inside was a job application, a résumé, a headshot, and a background check on Homer. I flipped through the pages. By the time I was done, I knew his blood type, his credit score, and his measurements.

"Nasty gave you this?" I guessed.

He nodded.

"But the *New Nautilus* didn't give it to her, did they?"

He shook his head.

I set the folder on the table and fanned out the pages. It made sense. Nasty would not have set us up with a person she didn't know. The *New Nautilus* might have offered Homer as our contact, but Nasty would have done her legwork to make sure he could be trusted.

And now he was dead.

"Maybe the lawsuit didn't go away. Depending on the size of it, the *New Nautilus* might have found a less common way to deal with the problem." I pantomimed a knife going into my chest, which was pretty close to the condition in which I'd found Homer's body.

Before Tex could respond, there was a knock on the door. "Mr. and Mrs. Templeton? It's Lenny. I'm here with your luggage." A second later, after an audible *click*, the door opened.

In one motion, I jammed the pages into the white folder and handed it to Tex. He returned it to the cookie cabinet. Fortunately for us, maneuvering a luggage cart stacked with suitcases wasn't an easy task, so by the time Lenny was inside our quarters, Tex and I looked like a married couple sharing the paper over our morning coffee.

"Good morning," Lenny said. "I'm sorry it took so long for me to get this to you. It's been one thing after another since we left Galveston."

Tex folded the paper and stood. "You need some help, mate?"

Mate?

"No, thanks. Okay if I stack it in your bedroom?"

"That's fine," I called out. I shot a glance at Tex, who had lost his edge of "I'm on vacation." Lenny pushed the cart into the bedroom, and I mouthed the word *Relax*.

A few seconds later, Lenny returned. He glanced at the

cantaloupe rind on the table. "Didn't the kitchen send up your breakfast pastry tray?"

"We didn't request one," Tex said.

"It's part of my contract," I said at the same time.

"I'll have it fixed for tomorrow. Is everything else okay? Do you need more towels or anything?"

I stood. "I'm sure all my husband needs is a change of clothes. Thank you, Lenny." I turned to Tex and made what I thought was a covert tip-the-man gesture.

Lenny held his hands up. "No tips, please. It's against company policy."

"Well, thank you all the same," I said.

Lenny left. Considering I had a collection of matching suitcases and Tex had just the one, it didn't surprise me that he remained at the dining room table while I went to our room to unpack. Tex's black rolling bag sat a few feet away from my luggage, as if Lenny didn't think our baggage should comingle. If only all metaphors were so accurate.

I yanked the top suitcase from the stack, set it on a luggage rack, then flipped the latches and opened it. Since first boarding the boat, our belongings had been moved enough times to leave the contents in a jumble, but what I saw inside the suitcase was the last thing I expected.

Two pillows had been jammed into the suitcase to fill it. Sandwiched between the pillows was a bulging cotton sack. I pulled the sack out and dumped the contents onto the bed, revealing jewelry, small electronics, and cash.

CHAPTER EIGHTEEN

"Hey, Tex, can you come look at something?" I stood rooted in place while waiting for confirmation that I wasn't hallucinating.

Tex came into the room and cursed. "Night, how much jewelry did you pack?"

"None," I said. "Actually, that's not true. I brought some earrings and flower pins. The jewelry I always wear."

"Then what's this?"

"I'm pretty sure the technical term is 'stolen goods.'"

Tex, who was in the middle of reaching for a necklace, froze with his arm extended toward the pile. "None of this is yours?"

"Look closely. Does any of it look like mine?"

Lying loosely in a tangle in my suitcase were strands of pearls, gold chains, pendants, and bracelets. There were pins and earrings and rings, a couple of wallets, and a fountain pen that didn't look cheap. Wedged into the side of the suitcase between the pillow and the interior wall was a wooden box. I couldn't see the contents from that angle, but I suspected they weren't inexpensive either.

"You said this trip allowed you to pack items you've never worn. Things you've picked up from estate sales over the years that don't fit your existing lifestyle. Are you sure this stuff wasn't in with the clothes you took out of storage? Maybe it was already in one of the many suitcases in your inventory and you grabbed the wrong one?"

With my back to the suitcase, I opened a desk drawer and removed a pen that was branded with the *New Nautilus* name and website. I turned back and lifted a strand of creamy pearls with a bright-gold clasp. A price tag from a boutique in Dallas that had opened last month was still attached to the lobster claw clasp, indicating that the pearls cost well into the five-figure range. "If the original owner of my vintage suitcase purchased this strand of pearls, she did so as a ghost."

I tipped the pen, and the necklace slid off into the pile. I dropped the pen onto the mattress and crossed my arms. "Not that I don't appreciate your ability to come up with more than one theory, but are you going to hang this on me?" I unfolded my arms and gestured toward the loot with a sweep of my arm. "None of this is vintage. It's all new. There are watches and handbags and designer wallets. There are three billfolds and two bulging envelopes marked with bank logos and whatever is in that box wedged into the side. I didn't pack this stuff."

Tex reached into his back pocket and pulled out a rubber glove. He slipped it on.

"Where did that come from?"

"We're here to investigate a crime. I told you I came prepared."

"That's not exactly what you said."

"It's what I meant." With his gloved hand, he extricated the box from the side of the suitcase. It was a watch box, partitioned into nine individual compartments with nine unique timepieces. Rolex. Cartier. Patek Phillippe. Omega. Breitling. The hits just kept on coming.

I jutted my chin toward the box. "That box is worth a couple hundred thousand dollars."

"Since when do you know watches?"

"I don't. I have a guy who knows watches."

I wasn't an expert on watches, but over the years of buying out estate sales, I'd come across more than one timepiece that held value to collectors. Because those watches weren't part of my business model, I sought an expert who told me what I had and, often, put me in touch with someone who wanted it. His knowledge had been so helpful that in time, we struck a deal. I offered the watches to him to sell, and he paid me a percentage of the sale price. Usually, the watches in question were Timex and Seiko, but when something of value came into my possession, we both did a little happy dance at the arrangement.

Judging from the names on the watch faces, the contents of this case would have earned a happy dance. Maybe more than one.

Tex set the box on the bedspread. He poked through the tangle of jewelry, sorting it loosely into piles. He then picked up a wallet and slid out an identification card. "Where's that passenger manifest Nasty gave us?"

"Out front. Wait here." I left him in our room, and I got the file from my handbag. "What's the name?"

"Ramirez," he said.

I scanned the list of names. "There's no Ramirez."

He set the wallet down and picked up another. "Check Bolger."

Once again, I scanned the list of names. "No Bolger."

Tex dropped the wallet onto the pile. He bent down and pulled up his pants leg, revealing a file folder wrapped around his calf and secured with a rubber band. He slid the band down and handed me the file. "Check in there."

"You do come prepared, don't you?"

"I'm used to being in tight spaces," he said.

I raised my eyebrows.

"I was talking about my space capsule. Jeez, Templeton, get your mind out of the gutter."

"Sorry, Captain Komarov. It won't happen again." I flattened Tex's hidden file against the console and opened it. Inside was a different list of passengers. I ran my finger down the list, stopping at Ramirez. "Ramirez is here."

"What about Bolger?"

"No. There's a Bogosian and a Boyle but no Bolger."

"Bogosian? You sure?"

I held the paper up for him to see. The list was alphabetized and went from Bogosian, Sam to Boyle, Daniel.

"Huh," he said.

"What?"

"Nothing important."

I tapped the sheet of paper. "What is this?"

"It's the itinerary for the previous cruise. The one with the theft."

"That means whoever stole from the guests never took their booty off the boat."

"Or it means somebody's onto us and planted this stuff to get us out of the picture." He pulled out his bat phone. "I'm calling Nasty."

The call didn't go through. Whatever data plan Tex had intended to keep us connected to the world we knew had left us in the lurch.

* * *

ACCORDING to the cruise ship itinerary, we were expected to reach Cozumel tomorrow morning. That gave us a full day on the ship. So much had happened yesterday in the brief amount of time since leaving Texas that I was tempted to hole up in our room and not leave until the trip was over.

There was a thing called overload, and I was dangerously near the tipping point.

But.

Since boarding the boat, we'd found a body, changed rooms three times, identified some suspicious behavior, and discovered a cache of loot that had been planted in our luggage. It was time to take a step back, figure out what we knew, and figure out what we didn't.

While Tex showered and changed into fresh clothes, I dug into my luggage, underneath several layers of shirtwaist dresses, for my sketchbook and a set of colored markers. I carried them to the kitchen and wrote out names of everyone we'd met. Thanks to a roll of hem tape that I kept in my overnight kit—because I came prepared too—I was able to hang them from one of the walls of our new quarters to assess the evidence. Tex joined me and we listed crimes and suspects, suspicious happenings, and anything else we felt we needed to explore. It wasn't a war room at the police station, but it would do.

"We have a body," I said. I tapped the sheet of paper that said *Homer*.

"Don't start with Homer. Start with the thefts. That's why we're here."

"But murder is a bigger crime than theft."

"We aren't here to investigate a murder."

"You don't expect me to believe you're going to look the other way while a body with a knife in it gets transported from Galveston to Cozumel and back."

As soon as I spoke the thought, I realized there was a much more troubling aspect to the jewelry planted in our luggage. "Our room," I said. "Someone had to get inside our original room to plant the jewelry in our luggage. That person must have found Homer's body in the bathtub."

CHAPTER NINETEEN

Tex stood by the wall of suspects. His dark-blond hair was a little longer than usual, and the front of it hung down on his forehead. He'd dressed in a white Lacoste shirt and khaki trousers. I didn't know Tex owned khaki trousers. His shirt was snug enough to show off his broad chest and defined arms. Since becoming the captain of the police force, he spent more time behind a desk than before, and with that came less physical movement and more doughnuts. He had added a layer of softness to his frame. The hard edges were still there but a little more difficult to see.

From his expression, he wasn't thrilled with what I'd figured out. I didn't believe for a moment that he hadn't already reached the same conclusion, probably in half the time, but to hear me say it aloud meant we had to deal with it.

If it was true that we were there to investigate a theft ring aboard the cruise ship, then discovering merchandise stolen from passengers on a previous cruise in our luggage—luggage that had been temporarily stored in a room with a murder victim that very few people on the ship were supposed to know about—made the investigation into the theft become an investigation into a homicide. Tex could pretend we were investigating one and not the other, but the two seemed inextricable.

"What if there aren't any burglaries on this trip?" I asked Tex.

He faced me but didn't speak right away. He was clearly thinking, processing, running a variety of possible answers through his mental computer.

There was a big difference in the way Tex and I reached conclusions. For most of my life, I had trusted people, until one day, that turned out very poorly for me. It was at the top of a ski slope, a romantic getaway with the man in my life at the time, the one I'd thought was my soulmate. With one sentence, he broke my heart. My response—to try to outski the implications of his words—left me with a torn ACL and a hefty deductible from my subsequent hospital stay. From that point on, my life had never been the same.

After my insurance benefits ran out, I went home to recover. As I slowly weaned myself off painkillers, I chose to move forward. I negotiated my way out of my lease, donated almost everything I owned to a women's shelter, and headed to Dallas, Texas. I had no connection to Dallas except a dislike of their football franchise. There was nothing about the city to lure me there except a plethora of affordably priced mid-century modern properties that were often featured in *Atomic Ranch* magazine. I might as well have closed my eyes and pointed at a map.

But because of that choice, because of the uniqueness of Dallas and my lack of history with the city, it felt like the perfect place for a fresh start. What I needed was a clean break from my life. My parents had died when I was in my early twenties, and now, with no family, no relationships, and no job of my own, I was untethered. A lifetime of watching Doris Day movies—an annual tradition with my family while growing up, thanks to me being born on the actress's birthday—trained me on mid-century design. It was the slimmest thing to hang my future on, but those movies and those memories kept me in touch with the belief that no matter how I felt after the breakup, I wasn't alone. If I followed my passion, I would attract the right people and start to build a new life.

I never, ever, *ever* could have predicted how that would unfold.

I'd invested my savings in a run-down apartment building where I lived as a resident. I met a handyman, Hudson, who felt like more than a freelance contact, though he repeatedly declined my offers to become a business partner. I adopted a puppy, Rocky, and started Mad for Mod, my interior design business. The money from the apartment building kept me afloat while I bought out estates ripe with original mid-century modern accessories and built-ins that new owners wanted to tear out. I went from a client here and there to a full schedule. I even had an office manager until Nasty poached her out from under me.

The thought of Nasty reminded me why we were there: a job. For the first time since Tex and I had met, we were expected to investigate something. Together.

It wasn't him investigating and me operating on the sidelines with an instinct for wrong place, wrong time. We were expected to operate as a team, yet less than a day after the cruise ship pulled away from the dock, Tex had established an undercover identity as a Russian cosmonaut, and I was suspected of having an affair.

We did not know how to operate as a team.

"Say that again?" Tex prompted.

I'd been so lost in thought that I nearly forgot what I said.

"About the burglaries," he added.

I took a moment to rewind my thoughts and get back to the conversation at hand.

"What if there aren't any burglaries on this trip? We're both acting like we were hired to catch the burglar, but what if Nasty never expected us to catch anybody? What if we're just here as a distraction? Nasty told us she needed a married couple. She could have put any one of her security bros on this ship to catch the burglar. She could have done it herself and gotten a vacation to boot. Why the cover story?"

"She told her client she was sending in two investigators posing as a married couple."

"Right. She told her client that. That doesn't mean she had to do it. It just means she alerted her client to the fact that a married couple who weren't what they seemed would be on the ship. If her client wants the thefts to stop, he wouldn't care who she sent. The cruise has insurance, and they already paid out. That means the passengers who all that stuff in my suitcase belonged to already got reimbursed for their belongings."

"Have you ever had that happen?"

"I've had my luggage go missing from an airplane. They have a standard policy for reimbursement. If you claim to have lost items of higher value than their insurance company covers, they require proof before they'll reimburse you."

"What proof?"

"Pictures of the contents of your luggage, maybe pictures

of you wearing the items to show you had them on the trip. It's never been a problem for me. I have more vintage clothes than I could use in ten lifetimes. If an airline loses one of my suitcases, I take their check and deposit it in my account."

Tex didn't dismiss my thoughts. He didn't tell me I wasn't making any sense or indicate that I was off somewhere in left field. He simply stood there, facing me, with our suspicious-behavior notes, torn from my sketchpad, taped to the wall behind him.

Without saying a word, he turned around and scanned his wall of notes. Then he reached up and pulled down the pages one by one.

"Wait!" I rushed forward and put my hands on his arm to stop him.

He crumpled the pieces of paper into balls and lobbed them toward the trash basket in the corner. He made every shot, a testament to how often Tex shot baskets of trash in his office at the precinct. Luca Dončić had nothing on him.

He turned around and put his hand on top of mine then gently removed my grip from his arm. He didn't release my hand. "We can't do this here."

"What are we doing?"

He used his free hand to point his thumb at the now-empty wall behind him. "This."

He held his finger to his lips, spun around, and tore the rest of the notes from the wall. He took my hand and led me to the bedroom. The suitcase filled with stolen jewelry that sat in the middle of the bedspread.

Tex passed the bed and opened the sliding doors. A damp breeze filtered into the room, catching the curtains and gently rustling the fabric. He stepped onto the balcony. I followed him. Two chairs and a table were there, but neither of us sat. I took my place next to him at the railing and stared out at the night sky. The ocean water was dark, near black, vaguely green where the boat sliced through it, thanks to exterior boat lights. Peace and tranquility as far as the eye could see. The only sounds were those of water lapping against the boat and a few gulls calling over our heads.

"Where are we, Night?"

"Is that a trick question?"

"We're in the Sanctuary, where we were moved after being assigned a room we never should have been given. None of this has been random."

I saw Tex's point. Someone had assigned us that very first room even though, according to more than one source, it shouldn't have been used for passengers. From that point on, we'd been at the mercy of someone else. Even after Lenny gave us the key cards to the luxury suite, we'd been without our luggage. It was starting to feel an awful lot like we were balls in an arcade game, pinging off bumpers willy-nilly.

"The crew all said our original room was supposed to be empty," I said. "But someone knew it wasn't. Someone saw an opportunity to frame us."

"Follow that thought."

"Somebody knows we're onto them."

Tex nodded. "What you said about the insurance policy is probably true. A cruise this size doesn't operate without a hefty policy. That means every person who claims to have been robbed is going to get a check to replace their loss if they haven't already. Insurance companies have standard rates for reimbursement, so unless a person can provide proof of what they had with them, they're all going to be reimbursed equally."

"That box of watches was probably worth more than the rest of the jewelry combined."

"Did you notice anything unusual about it?"

"The fact that it was safely tucked into the side of the suitcase instead of being tossed in an empty pillowcase like the rest of the contents?"

"Right. I'd sure like to see a list of what was reported as missing."

* * *

WE DIDN'T HAVE a lot to do. Reporting the loot meant letting someone know we knew about the thefts, and without a contact on the boat, every person we'd met had been slotted into the suspicious-behavior column. While Tex tried to reach Nasty, I tried to reach Imogene to check on Rocky. Neither of our calls connected.

My late bedtime from the previous night caught up with me, and after unpacking, I fell asleep. It was out of character, but when Tex covered me in the thin sheet, I was too tired to protest. I vaguely remembered him pulling the curtains closed, blocking the sunlight.

I woke two hours later. I didn't know that at first. What I knew was that I was alone. After tossing back the covers, I looked for a clock, handily finding one in the box of stolen watches. I redressed in my mock turtleneck and yellow skort and went out front. Tex was gone.

The peaceful sounds of our journey had been replaced by laughter. A perky female voice announced a wine tasting at two thirty and a bourbon bar at five over the ship's loudspeaker. If I was lucky, maybe my audience would be soused by the time I took the stage.

I helped myself to a cheese Danish from a pastry tray that had been delivered while I napped, made a second cup of coffee in the Nespresso machine, then sat at the table and flipped through the notes Tex had left. Behind the pages torn from my sketch pad, he'd added the passenger manifest from the previous cruise. I was about to close the folder when two names jumped out at me: Meg and Mavis Stork.

I swallowed my mouthful and chased it with a swig of coffee, all the while thinking about what that meant. I already knew the Stork sisters were cruise regulars, but this manifest put them on the very same cruise where passengers had been robbed.

Which meant they could have been victims... or they could be responsible.

CHAPTER TWENTY

IF EITHER OF THE STORK SISTERS WAS INVOLVED IN EITHER OF the crimes we knew about, then they were dangerous. I wasn't about to sit around waiting for Tex to return with information. At a minimum, he needed to know what I knew.

I set my plate in the sink, slathered myself in sunscreen, then slipped on a yellow vinyl visor and white sunglasses. I took a magnetic key card from the counter and left. Thanks to Tex's diagram, I knew the direct path to the pool. I followed the hallway until I detected the familiar scent of chlorine then emerged from the stairwell onto the deck.

If the scene in front of me was any indication, the majority of the passengers didn't know there'd been a murder yesterday. The real estate girlfriends were in the pool, one in a skimpy bikini, the other in a one-shoulder red maillot. They swatted a multicolored inflatable ball back and forth with their boyfriends, who seemed to have gotten over the trauma of being on a nostalgia cruise, though the aggression with which they swatted the beach ball back and forth suggested they'd found an outlet for their sublimated anger. On the deck nearby, two thin men with shaggy hair and bare chests slept in lounge chairs next to a third, who kept his eyes on the couples in the pool while tapping out a beat on the chair with a pair of drumsticks.

Beyond the pool was a bar. Lenny, the boatswain, was operating a blender filled with something frothy and blue. A line of people stood by the bar with empty cups. So far, the main attraction appeared to be the bottomless booze.

As I stood on the deck and cataloged people, the inflatable pool ball blew over to me. I caught it handily and was about to toss it back when I saw something I wished I hadn't.

Tex was on the opposite side of the pool deck, talking to Mavis.

Today, the head of my fan club wore a white T-shirt that said CRUISE CONTROL over her bathing suit. Her name necklace was crooked and stuck to her brown skin. She held a cup of something blue and had her head cocked, slurping and listening as Tex spoke. I needed a way to let him know what I'd discovered, but Mavis didn't know Tex as my husband. She knew him as a Russian cosmonaut. That dictated how I crashed their conversation.

I advanced toward the end of the pool, then water splashed onto my feet. I forgot that I held the inflatable pool ball, and I tossed it back. The man who caught it said thanks and slammed the ball at his buddy's head. It bounced off and came back to me, and this time, I spiked it toward the girlfriends.

I left the battling couples and beat a path toward the bar. Tex had his back to me, but Mavis handled my arrival with aplomb.

"Doris! Perfect timing. I was just asking Captain Komarov about life in space."

Tex faced me, and I smiled a smile that I hoped captured polite interest and maybe a little I-can't-wait-to-hear-this.

"My name isn't Doris," I told him. "It's Madison." I held out my hand.

"How could I forget?" He took my hand and kissed the back of it.

"Such a gentleman," Mavis said to no one in particular.

"May I get you a beverage?" Tex asked me.

"I'd love a water," I said.

"Get her a tiki drink." Mavis raised her blue drink to me. "There's hardly any alcohol in them."

Tex excused himself, which was not what I'd wanted, but I knew he would return. Mavis didn't wait for him to get out of earshot before she said, "You'd never know he was Russian. He doesn't even have an accent."

"That's probably due to his time on the space station." I said it as a joke, but when she turned her full attention to me, I backpedaled to maintain Tex's cover. "He must spend time with other members of the space program. You know how it's easy to pick up an accent after watching a movie?"

"That's never happened to me."

I did the only thing I could think of. I adopted my best Doris Day–impersonator voice and said, "Really?" I chuckled, mimicking Doris's throaty laugh. "It happens to me all the time."

Mavis's eyes lit up with delight. "Oh, that's good! You're good! I can't wait to tell my sister." She put her hand on my wrist and pulled me close. "Here he comes. Try it out on him."

Tex returned, holding three frothy blue beverages

wedged in a triangle. I took one of the cups, and Mavis took another. The female voice on the loudspeaker ran through the day's activities, ending with a plug for my set in the Nautilus Shell at eight.

"Captain, you *are* coming to see our Doris sing tonight, aren't you?" Mavis asked.

"Wouldn't miss it." He raised his beverage to his lips, and that was when I noticed it. Tex, who'd told me he didn't bring a watch, now wore one.

It wasn't just any watch either. At a glance, the face of the watch was crowded with numbers and markings. It was black, and even numbers were printed in gold: two, four, eight, ten, fourteen, sixteen, twenty, twenty-two, twenty-four. Additional numbers in white marked a ring around the face, like a round ruler. I squinted and read the words in the center of the watch face: BREITLING GENEVE COSMONAUTE.

What the—?

Tex noticed me staring at his wrist. He switched hands and stuck his left hand in his pocket. I followed the watch until it wasn't visible anymore then looked at Tex's face. We shared one of those wordless communications we had perfected over the years. If there'd been a transcript of our thoughts, it might have gone:

Me: Did you "borrow" evidence—

Tex: Later, Night.

Me: Later, indeed, Captain, but not the way you think!

If Mavis noticed any of that, she didn't respond. She sipped from her drink and took in the crowd. Knowing I couldn't press Tex on his decision to take a stolen watch from the loot stashed in my luggage, I had to play it cool. I raised my drink to my lips and sipped, watching Mavis watch everybody else.

The burn of alcohol was overwhelming. I raised my glass to spit the frothy blue back into my cup, but Tex elbowed me. He shook his head imperceptibly and glanced at my beverage. I forced myself to swallow. The burn traveled down my throat, and I coughed. I searched Tex's face. His eyebrows dropped low over his eyes. Tex was up to more than just impersonating a cosmonaut.

Until Mavis left, Tex and I were destined to play our two respective roles. "Is your sister feeling any better?" I asked Mavis.

"She's fine," Mavis said. "She was up at the crack of dawn to do yoga on the lido deck. For the life of me, I'll never understand morning people, but she claims it helps her start her day."

"Do you have anything special planned for today?"

Mavis gave me her full attention. "Just lounging around the pool with a few of these," she said, raising her cup. She pulled the straw toward her and took a long swig.

The blue liquid rose into the straw as she sucked on it, and I waited for her to react to the strength of the drink the way I had. But Mavis didn't seem to think anything of the drink's alcohol content. She swallowed a few gulps then released a satisfying "ah."

"We paid for the all-inclusive package. Got to get my money's worth! See you tonight, Doris. And Captain, don't forget, you promised me a signature!" She grinned and headed to the back of the line at the bar.

Tex and I were alone in a crowd. I stood in front of him and said, "We need to talk."

"Not here."

"Lead the way, Captain."

He scowled. I raised my eyebrows. He turned around and walked toward the exit, and I followed.

We reached the hallway, and the sounds of guests at the pool faded into a low din. Tex turned back to me, and I grabbed his wrist and held it up. He clenched his fist, and to anyone watching, it might have looked as if we were engaged in a struggle.

It was just our luck that someone *was* watching. Someone who chose that moment to play knight in shining armor.

CHAPTER TWENTY-ONE

"Hey!" Lenny called out to us. "Leave her alone!"

Tex and I froze. My hand was on his wrist, and his arm was raised. We looked in Lenny's direction. "It's not like it looks." Tex relaxed his arm, and suddenly, I was holding the weight of it. The rugged watch was rough under my fingers. There was one other explanation for our body language. "I was just checking the time." I gave Lenny my brightest smile and shifted my hand to reveal Tex's watch face. Tex flinched. We didn't know whether Lenny had played a role in the thefts or the murder, but if he saw the stolen cosmonaut watch on Tex and recognized it, he might have questions.

Lenny's eyes moved from my face to Tex's arm then back up to Tex's face. He didn't appear to have a reaction to the watch and didn't appear to see it as anything other than a watch. He was far enough away that he might not be able to see the crowded watch face, and that worked for us—until it didn't.

"Where did you get that?" Lenny asked Tex.

"My watch?"

Lenny nodded. "It is strongly recommended that people leave timepieces at home. It helps people acclimate to the feeling of vacation faster. No clock to punch, no hard times to follow. The activities on the boat blend into each other, so there's no firm schedule."

Just then, the female voice came over the loudspeaker. "Welcome, cruisegoers! We'll be docking in Cozumel tomorrow morning, so enjoy your time today! Perfect your swing at our new putting range on the lido deck or relax with drinks by the pool on the mezzanine. If you prefer aquatic life, visit our glass bottom, or try your luck with a mermaid sighting. And don't forget to join us in the Nautilus Shell for a special performance tonight at eight!"

"Maybe someone should tell the announcer that the ship is not supposed to run according to a schedule," I told Lenny.

His face shaded pink. "She wasn't supposed to say that."

"Who makes the announcements?" Tex asked.

"Willow. We're all pitching in to cover the purser responsibilities now that Homer…" Lenny's voice trailed off, and the color in his face morphed from pink to green.

"Who else knows about Homer?" I asked.

"After I told the captain, he had a meeting with the core crew."

"Who's that?"

Lenny, who had no reason to think Tex and I were anything other than the talent and her manager husband who'd happened to find a body while on the boat, didn't give me the answer I sought.

"We're all under instructions not to talk about what happened. I know you know, but from this point on, I think it's best if you try to forget."

"Forget that there's a dead man in the bathtub of our original room?"

Lenny glanced over both shoulders. "I shouldn't be talking about this."

My grip on Tex had relaxed without me thinking about it, and he slung his arm around my shoulders. "My wife is having a hard time dealing with what happened."

"I thought you said she was a true-crime junkie?" Lenny asked.

"It's one thing when you hear about it," I said. "It's another when you're the one who finds the body."

Lenny nodded as if that were a plausible explanation. Neither Tex nor I told him it wasn't my first time, or even my second, of finding a body. In fact, the number of bodies I had reported in Dallas was now in the double digits. Maybe I was a true-crime junkie; maybe I needed to enter rehab.

But not today.

"I suppose the show must go on," I said to neither man in particular. Tex's arm tightened around my shoulders.

"You're due in the Nautilus Shell at seven thirty for a sound check. You can get in at seven if you want to bring your costumes."

"If we're not supposed to adhere to a schedule, how am I supposed to know when it's seven o'clock?"

Lenny pointed at Tex's arm. "Your husband's wearing a watch. Might as well use it."

* * *

TEX'S and my time on the ship was earmarked for snooping, but my upcoming performance was a monolith in the center of that otherwise clear schedule. Besides that, I was hungry.

One sip of booze wasn't enough to make me drunk, but I was still in need of water.

After Lenny left us, Tex and I strolled toward one of the ship's restaurants. I brought him up to speed with what I'd discovered.

"Both Meg and Mavis were on the last cruise. I though they were innocent Doris Day fans, but it's possible all of that is an act."

"You're a Doris Day fan. Do they strike you as inauthentic?"

"No. I mean, to the casual viewer, Doris Day movies are a time capsule that lack ethnic diversity, but you could blame that on Hollywood. I connected with her personal story. They could have too."

"I thought you liked her because you were born on her birthday."

I grinned. "That's how she landed on my radar, but then when I learned about her life, it became so much more than that."

"What about her life?"

"She was never supposed to become an actress. She was a dancer, but she broke both legs in a car accident before she turned fifteen. She became a singer and married a band leader who started beating her the second day of their marriage. Her third husband mismanaged her estate and left her with nothing."

Tex whistled. "Do I want to ask about husband number two?"

"Number two and number four didn't stick. But she smiled through everything life threw at her and kept on going. It's that, her willingness to believe that something better was around the corner no matter how bad things seemed, that made me see her as more than the sum of her movies. There was a time when people thought she symbolized everything wrong with America, but her friendship with Rock Hudson while he struggled with AIDS and her work for animals has helped people see her legacy differently, to recognize that her image was a product of a studio system. Even she said it was more fake than any film part she played."

"When you first met the Storks, what did they say?"

I thought back to that first conversation. "They knew the names of her movie characters and her costars, but that's barely scratching the surface."

Talking about the Stork sisters distracted me from my singing gig temporarily, but not enough to push it from my mind. It didn't help that the two women who'd been my biggest fans were now squarely on my suspect list.

"You hungry?" Tex asked.

"Every time I think about getting on that stage tonight, I lose my appetite."

"You'll be fine," he said. "Let's get some shrimp cocktail."

Tex led me to the Starboard Café, and before long, we were seated across from each other next to a wall of windows. It was a little after three, and the restaurant was mostly empty. Other cruise passengers were scattered throughout but not near us. I spotted a big-boned woman in a colorful muumuu. I remembered the green-pink-and-white print from when I'd systematically let myself into the guest rooms yesterday. The print was cheerful and perfect for a cruise, and somewhere in the bottom of one of my suitcases was a similar garment. It was too bad muumuus had gone out of fashion; the style was among the most comfortable items a person could wear and it was "one size fits most." What's not to love?

Tex ordered for us—"Four shrimp cocktails, bring them two at a time, two bottles of sparkling water"—and reached across the table for my hand. The gesture took me by surprise until I remembered we were playing the role of married couple. I squeezed his fingertips.

"Did I ever tell you about the time I impersonated a rodeo clown?"

"I believe you've kept that story to yourself."

"The manager of the Fort Worth Rodeo suspected someone of doping the broncos. There was an internal investigation, but nobody was caught. Bronco busting is a dangerous sport, and it was largely considered to be the price of participating, but after three different riders were almost killed, it was tipping from rodeo sport into blood sport. Ticket sales were up, but at what cost?"

He still held my hand across the table, and I didn't let go. Ever since Tex's sister had moved to Dallas five months ago, I'd had a window into his life before me, but he didn't often share details about his past investigations. I didn't think he was hiding anything but that he had learned to compartmentalize that part of his life. Plus, once an investigation was closed, he was on to the next. Cops didn't spend a lot of time sitting around reliving cases they'd cracked. No matter what the closure rate, a murder was still a murder. Keeping the details of the seedier aspects of humanity behind an internal fortress was how Tex managed to have a life outside of it.

There were numerous jokes I could make about Tex at a rodeo. Some might say he'd been born to participate in one, but this didn't feel like the time for easy jokes at his expense.

"What happened?" I prompted.

"One of my buddies was on the Fort Worth police force. He suspected the manager was involved in the doping scandal and that the police investigation had been arranged to create the perception of integrity and to get them a clean slate. He asked if I'd be willing to go in undercover to see if there was anything there."

"You grew up around horses, didn't you?"

He nodded. "The rodeo circuit is small. If I arrived out of nowhere and knew too much, it would raise suspicions. We worked out a cover and a backstory, and I went in as a clown."

I tried to picture Tex in colorful patchwork rags, pumping up a crowd wanting to be entertained by the show. "Is that like being a carnival barker?"

"That's part of it. The other part is getting into a barrel and letting a bronco roll you around an arena."

"Sounds dangerous."

He tipped his head from side to side as if considering and agreeing, conceding that maybe it was and maybe it wasn't but that the possible danger wasn't the point of his story.

Sensing that, I asked, "Was it worth it?"

Tex had been looking over my head, but he refocused his attention on me. "The owner of the broncos was injecting the bulls with a steroid that supercharges their nervous system. He was basically riling them up right before he released them into the field of play. That bull is already wild. He's already a force of opposition. The dope made him into a killer. I caught the owner with the smoking hypodermic needle in his hand. He's been banned from the rodeo circuit for life, and the integrity of the sport is intact."

"What about your clown duties?"

"The show must go on." The first round of shrimp cocktail arrived, and Tex released my hand and ate a shrimp. After he swallowed, he said, "Night, your cover is a device to get to the bottom of a bigger crime. It's like using a wrench to fix a sink. We're here because of that cover, but if we do our job, after we leave this ship, nobody is going to remember how you sang. They're going to remember how a police captain and his decorator girlfriend posed undercover on a ship and exposed a theft ring and a murderer. Don't get bogged down with nerves over a performance that doesn't matter. It's a tool, that's all."

"Have you gone undercover a lot?"

"More than once. I can tell you're nervous about possibly embarrassing yourself tonight. Not much more embarrassing than dressing up as a rodeo clown and letting a juiced-up bull knock you around in a barrel. I don't share that story with a lot of people."

"I appreciate it, Captain." And I did. It was in these moments with Tex that I saw what the rest of the world did not, how deeply he cared about truth and justice and—especially in the case of the rodeo circuit—the American way. Tex's one driving force was to find out who committed a crime. I loved him for that. Deep passions would take us to places we couldn't always predict, and I would rather spend my time with a person with their own passions than a person with none. I knew it led him into dangerous situations, ones he might always keep to himself, and maybe it was my quest to live a full life that allowed me to look past that and know we had a connection. "Thank you for sharing your most embarrassing story with me."

"Not my most embarrassing," he said easily. "That would be the time I took the stage for Ladies' Night at Jumbo's."

CHAPTER TWENTY-TWO

Tex and I wasted over an hour in the restaurant, sharing innocuous stories and reliving a few of our shared memories while splitting a thick slice of key lime pie. Our corner of the restaurant was tucked away from prying eyes and eavesdropping ears, and it felt good to just be myself, Madison Night, for a brief interlude.

After we finished our shrimp cocktail lunch, we went in separate directions. When we'd first boarded the ship, it might have made sense for us to play the part of the doting couple, but now that Tex had an alternate persona and I was suspected of having an affair on the side, we had a better cover when we were apart. Tex went to his cosmonaut quarters to check on the hallway where Homer's body was, and I went in search of Persephone.

From everything I'd learned thus far, Persephone was the most suspicious person on the ship. She was the decorator, and that gave us something in common. But at every turn, I questioned her design choices. Tex wrote them off by saying that the style popular in the mid-century probably wasn't her favorite era of design, which I thought was a shame, but it wasn't so easy for me to overlook her apparent lack of taste. Something about her didn't add up.

I figured a good cover story would be to arrive with my costumes in tow, so while Tex went his way, I went to the room. I took two garment bags of what I'd considered to be performance attire and left.

My plan was thwarted by Willow, who called after me in the hallway.

"Mrs. Templeton!"

I turned and faced the first officer. In her crew uniform, with her short hair tucked away under a cap, she had a boyish appearance.

"I've been looking all over for you." She put her hands on her waist and bent over, breathing heavily. I got the feeling her "looking all over" had involved a fair bit of running.

"Is something wrong?"

She looked up. "It's about your performance tonight."

"Oh?" I shifted the garment bags from one arm to the other. From the moment Tex and I had unpacked the car and boarded the boat, someone else had been in charge of our luggage, and I hadn't realized until just then how heavy those two bags were. Spangles, as Bob Mackie called them, weren't for sissies. But if Willow was there with the news that my singing performance had been canceled, I wasn't going to complain about a couple of garment bags.

Willow straightened and kept her hand on her side.

"Are you okay?"

"Side stitch."

I set the garment bags on the ground and unzipped the one on top, untangled a hanger from a dress, and held it out to her. "Try to break this."

"Huh?"

I put my hands on the hanger and pretended to bend it. "Like this. It'll make the side stitch go away."

Willow took the hanger and applied muscle to it. It was a coral wooden arc with a hook jutting out the top of it, one of many vintage hangers in my possession. The wood snapped under Willow's pressure. Her eyes widened, and she looked up. "I broke it."

"It's okay. I have hundreds of them at home." I reached out and took the broken hanger pieces from her. "How's your side stitch?"

She cocked her head and put her hand on her waist again, that time flexing and twisting. "It's gone. That's a great trick!"

"Happy to help." I stuck the hanger back into the garment bag only because there were no trash bins in the hallway. When I picked up my bag again, the weight of it shifted, and the bag bulged at the bottom.

"Let me carry those." Willow came toward me and grabbed my bags before I could protest. "Where are you headed?"

"I was on my way to the Nautilus Shell. You mentioned something about my set tonight?"

"There's been a change of schedule. Instead of you starting at eight, the captain wants you to start at five and sing during dinner."

"That's less than an hour away!"

"Right. We can push it a little, but you need to get there now. You'll finish your second set by seven, and the room will be reset for the Tossed Pebbles."

"I thought they were performing by the pool?"

"There's a chance of a storm tonight, so the captain told us to move them indoors."

"I have a better idea. Why not let them take over my spot?"

"We can't. There's a couple of regulars who said the whole reason they're here is because of you. Besides, if we make any radical changes to our itinerary after departing, we're at risk of losing our cruise accreditation."

"Moving my set up by three hours isn't considered radical?"

"No."

It figured. I was *this close* to getting out of the spotlight, and Meg and Mavis Stork were the ones keeping me locked in. I had a strong suspicion I would be singing to an audience of two, but like Tex said about the rodeo, the show must go on. "Fine. Let's go."

"Go where?"

"To the Nautilus Shell. I'd like some time to get acclimated to the room."

I led the way and, like the diva I pretended to be, allowed Willow to carry my garment bags. As I headed toward the end of the hallway, she called me back.

"Mrs. Templeton? Didn't anybody tell you about the shortcut?"

I whirled around. "What shortcut?"

She tipped her head toward a door in the hallway. "We keep this room vacant. There's a door on the front and back of it, and if you cut through here, you'll be in the same hallway as the Nautilus Shell. Hand me your key card. It should work."

I felt a mixture of curiosity and reluctance, but Willow's right hand was outstretched—her left was buried somewhere under the folds of the garment bags—so I let the scales tip in favor of curiosity and placed my key card in her palm. She waved it in front of the door, and the latch released. She tipped her head toward the door, and again, I led the way.

The room was empty. It had no bed, no desk, no chair, no luggage rack. It was simply an empty space. I passed through the room and opened the door on the other side before arriving in the same hallway as the nightclub.

"Are there always shortcuts like this on the ship?"

Willow looked sheepish. "It depends on how booked we are. If this cruise had sold out, Persephone would have had to decorate this room for guests."

"But when the ship is only partially booked like this cruise?"

"Normally, we leave one or two guest rooms open like this one, but it was easier to leave an entire wing of rooms empty this time, so the guests are all pretty much in the same general area."

"I see." And I did. Knowledge of the ship's shortcuts would allow a person to get from point A to point B faster than expected. It would also allow a person to be someplace they shouldn't, commit a crime, and get to another part of the ship fast enough to create the illusion of an alibi. While Tex, Lenny, and I had been on the lido deck with Homer's body, the rest of the crew was assembled on the mezzanine, greeting people as they boarded the boat. The only people I knew of who *weren't* on the mezzanine were Lenny, who'd been with us, and Jennifer, who had been in the ocean nearby. Their individual locations could serve as alibis or opportunities. That new knowledge expanded the suspect pool.

Willow and I arrived at the Nautilus Shell. The door was propped open. Since last night, the room had been transformed. Persephone had installed the mural on the far wall. At a glance, I knew she had miscalculated the placement of several pieces, and it bothered me to know I would have to stare at her errors from my perch on stage.

"Do you want these in the back?" Willow asked, holding up my bags.

"Sure."

She left me out front. Round tables that seated four were positioned throughout the room. Each table, covered in a white tablecloth, held a small plastic vase with a daisy. Gold cane chairs were tilted against each table, with a winding path between them.

I approached a table. Aside from the daisy in the centerpiece, nothing about the layout said Doris Day or 1966 or mid-century modern. It seemed even more obvious that Persephone had phoned in her job now that I knew she'd had half as many rooms to decorate as usual. She was at the top of my list of suspicious characters and not just because of her lack of decorating vision. Something about her didn't line up.

The door at the back of the room opened, and several people dressed similarly in white shirts, black trousers, and black neckties came in, each carrying a silver serving tray. They set the trays up on a row of tables I hadn't seen along the rear wall. A man in a chef's coat followed them with a lighter and a bag of small cans of Sterno. He lit each can, placed it under a tray, and moved on to the next.

I walked up to the group. "What's this?"

"Dinner," one of the waiters said.

"It's a buffet?"

He shrugged.

"Mrs. Templeton?"

I was getting used to the sound of Willow calling my

name. I turned toward the stage. "People are heading this way. You should probably get changed before any of them get here."

"Of course."

Every time someone mentioned my set, I felt a fleet of butterflies release in my chest. I remembered what Tex had told me about his turn as a rodeo clown, and I steeled my nerves. I'd sung Doris Day's songbook hundreds of times in the shower, in the studio, and in the car. I was letting stage fright get to me. Singing should be the easiest thing I did on the entire trip.

Backstage, a small vase of white daisies like the ones out front sat on a table with a card of instructions for operating the stereo system.

I changed into a turquoise dress with silver-sequined scrolls on the surface. The dress had a sweetheart neckline, long sleeves, and a narrow skirt with a thigh-high slit. It was from the estate of Addison Nigh. Addison was a once-popular jazz singer on the Dallas nightclub circuit, and about a year ago, our lives had intertwined in an unexpected way. I hadn't had much of an excuse to unpack her gowns since acquiring her estate, not until the cruise. Four of the five dresses I'd packed for my performances had come from her closet.

I slipped into a pair of silver shoes and buckled them at my ankles. The heels were low, but I was used to wearing Keds, so they might as well have been stilettos. I strode back and forth a few times to get the feel of them while reviewing my set list. Despite all the booze that had been freely flowing during the day, my backstage was remarkably dry.

As I paced, Persephone came back there. "You can start whenever you're ready."

"There won't be an introduction?"

"This isn't a residence in Vegas. You get an hour, a little more if the crowd wants an encore. The Tossed Pebbles will set their stage when you're done, and we've got a crowd waiting for them."

At least there were no doped-up bulls waiting to charge me.

I gave Persephone a minute to return to her seat. The stereo system was set up along the far wall, visible from the stage. I pressed Play. I adopted Doris's cheerful confidence, and I strode out to the center of the stage and hit my mark: an *X* taped onto the floor in blue painter's tape. My opening song was "Bright and Shiny," and the music would provide my singing cue. But it wasn't the music that marked my performance. It was an explosion that came from the stereo system beside me.

CHAPTER TWENTY-THREE

THE SHOCK OF THE EXPLOSION WAS ENOUGH TO KEEP ME FROM missing my singing cue. Sparks flew out of the stereo system. The burst of fire fizzled to a flicker. Tex charged the stage and moved me away from the burst. Two waiters from the back of the room ran forward to help. The audience, all ten of them, recoiled at the apparent equipment malfunction.

Doris Day's voice distorted through the speakers. I stood rooted in place while my small audience stared, probably wondering if this was part of the show. Another burst of sparks shot out of the stereo system, a display that would have enchanted children at a Memorial Day picnic but did nothing to calm my already fried nerves.

I went backstage to where the system was plugged in. Two wires were twisted together around a small black box. I touched the box and instantly pulled my hand back. It was too hot to touch.

Tex saw the same thing that I did. He grabbed the electrical cord and yanked it out of the socket. Sparks flew through the air but burned out before landing on anything they could ignite.

The backstage was silent, but the room out front buzzed with the response of the guests and employees.

"What happened?" I asked Tex.

He picked up a rag from a nearby bucket and used it to lift the black box and look at the back of it. "Somebody tampered with this."

"How many years of detective school did it take you to make that deduction?" I asked with an uncharacteristic burst of sarcasm.

"Night, don't."

"Don't what? That system was rigged to blow when I started my set. If I'd never pushed that power button, it would not have blown up. You're a cop, Tex. You're used to people trying to kill you. The performance nerves are bad enough, but this whole 'accident' targeted me."

Tex set the stereo down. We stared at each other with a barrier of hostility and fear between us. It didn't seem to matter that we tried to be careful, that we kept our sleuthing escapades to regular hours, or that we were legitimately there to expose a crime thanks to Nasty's arrangement. Someone here, on this ship, had rigged the stereo system to blow when I took the stage. It was personal, and there was no other way to see it.

"Excuse me, Mrs. Templeton?" Persephone said from the side of the stage. Her face was ashen. "I radioed Lenny and told him what happened. He's having dinner moved to the theater level, where the Tossed Pebbles are going to play an unplugged set."

"The people out front are okay with that?" Tex asked.

"There weren't that many of them." To her credit, she didn't gloat.

Persephone left us. Her unexpected arrival had served as a reset button on the tension between me and Tex. Alone again, we stared at each other. My nerves were settling, and I remembered that as long as I was on this ship, there was only one person I could trust. I was about to apologize for my outburst when Tex held up his finger. He crept to the side of the stage and looked out into the room. I scooped up the clothes I'd left strewn on the sofa and shoved them into my garment bag then zipped it up and hoisted it over my shoulder. I scanned the rest of the room, looking for a clue as to what had happened back here, and joined Tex out front.

The room had been vacated, and the buffet at the back of the room was gone. The only things left were empty round tables and gold chairs. More than half of the chairs were still tipped up toward the table, which told me Persephone had been polite when she commented on the number of people who had come to my singing debut.

The door to the kitchen opened, and a waiter poked his head in. He saw us and called out, "The buffet's been moved to the theater level."

Tex thanked him for the info. There was no point revealing we already knew why.

Tex carried my bags to the Sanctuary. We passed a few guests we hadn't met yet, and I was happy with the anonymity. I pulled out my key card and scanned us into our room then turned to Tex to apologize for my outburst.

He spoke first. "I think Persephone heard you call me a cop."

"When?"

"When we first went backstage. Your voice rose. You

called me a cop and said I was used to people trying to kill me."

I put my hands on my hips. "Are you seriously going to use this moment to tell me I blew our cover, Captain Komarov? Besides, you called me Night."

"When?"

"Right before I blew your cover. You said, 'Night, don't.'"

He appeared to think about that. "It could be your stage name."

"One would think we'd have put it into play by now."

He draped my garment bag across the dining room table, next to the bowl of fresh fruit. I sat down on a barstool and looked up at Tex. "One would also think Nasty would have given us a second contact on the ship," I added.

"What happened tonight was a warning. Somebody knows we're onto them. It's too risky for us to keep digging. For the rest of this cruise, we're done."

"What about Nasty?"

"Nasty will understand."

The floor-to-ceiling curtains were open, revealing the dark-blue sky, the near-full moon, and an abundance of stars, brighter than I remembered them being back home in Dallas.

Tex left me sitting on the barstool and went into the living area. He pulled out his bat phone and scrolled through something then docked the phone in a docking station provided by the ship. A few seconds later, Frank Sinatra was serenading us with "The Summer Wind." Before we could argue any more about who said what, who was trying to kill me, and what we would do next, we dropped all our identities and enjoyed the moment.

THE GLASS BOTTOM HOAX

* * *

THANKS to either the fresh air or the stress of the trip, I slept until seven the next morning. When I woke, the bed was empty. I found Tex playing solitaire in the spacious living room.

"Morning, Night," Tex said.

I held up my hand. "Please. No names."

He nodded and followed me to the kitchen. I brewed two mugs of coffee and handed him one. "It's a rare morning when I outsleep you."

"You had a stressful night." He hooked his elbow around my neck and pulled me toward him then kissed my temple. "The ship's going to dock in Cozumel in about an hour. We should come up with a plan."

The cruise itinerary sat on the center of the table, and I pulled it toward me. Most of my anticipation—rather, my anxiety—had been building toward last night's performance, and I hadn't thought too much about what came next. In the abstract, I knew that once I got through my performance, it was smooth sailing—or it should have been if Tex and I hadn't found a body, been set up with stolen loot in our luggage, or been the target of a vandalized stereo system.

If I didn't know any better, I would say Nasty had withheld some details about the job.

I scanned the schedule for the day. The ship was supposed to dock at eight o'clock. A map included in our orientation package briefly laid out the area where we would arrive and also detailed a few of the activities we could enjoy while there. The main event, organized by the cruise company, was a group wedding on the beach in the afternoon. The ceremony was scheduled for three, allowing time both before and after for guests to explore the island.

In addition to the wedding on the beach, there was a putting green, a private Jeep tour through Jade Cavern, a snorkeling adventure, and a shuttle to a touristy shopping destination. Considering we would be in Cozumel for only ten hours, the options were numerous.

"We could divide and conquer," I said. "We wouldn't have to worry about our cover stories if we aren't together."

"I don't like that idea. Not after what happened last night."

Tex had a point, and it had nothing to do with whose suggestion was better. There was danger all around us, and we were no closer to knowing which way to look.

"If we stick together, we're going to have to remember who thinks what about us. Meg and Mavis think you're a space man. Persephone thinks I'm cheating on you. Lenny knows we know about Homer's body, and the rest of the crew thinks we're the Templetons."

"It sure would be nice to have another contact on this ship. I don't trust any of them."

In the end, we decided to be ourselves—with a caveat: no names. If the Stork sisters saw us together, they would assume they were witness to a budding cruise ship romance, but nobody else would think twice.

I dressed in a sleeveless white cotton frock with a fitted bodice and sweetheart neckline. The full skirt swirled around my legs, and the cotton was dotted with appliques of flowers. It came from the estate of Sandra Ann Conine Fields, who had worn it for her wedding in 1969. The hem of the dress had discolored with age, but the whimsy of the daisy appliques made the dress too precious to toss. I'd had a local tailor hem it to just below my knees, which gave it a playful vibe. I slipped on white Keds and packed my sunscreen, sunglasses, and wallet in a raffia bag with coordinating daisies on the side. My last touch was a straw hat that kept my pale face in shade.

Once again, Tex's choice of attire surprised me. He wore a loose white dress shirt with white linen trousers and white canvas deck shoes. Unlike me, he sported a tan, which provided a stark contrast. His wrist was bare.

From the view in our bedroom, I saw the Cozumel harbor. We left our cabin and followed the flow of people congregating by the exits. I threaded my fingers through Tex's, and he squeezed my hand. Whatever happened for the rest of the trip, we were in it together.

The luster of me being part of the talent on the ship had tarnished thanks to last night's botched performance, and whatever popularity I'd had the first twenty-four hours on the boat had transferred to the Tossed Pebbles. The Rolling Stones tribute band had picked up an entourage—along with mimosas—and the group filled out the front of the line. Unlike me, the band members went by their stage names, and their fans had no problem calling them Mick, Keith, Ronnie, and Charlie. Tex and I stood back and let other guests pass before us. I couldn't speak for Tex's motivation, but I wanted a chance to see everybody one last time before they had a chance to make a break for it.

If someone didn't return to the ship, they would be leaving a giant Guilty sign behind.

The *New Nautilus* had partnered with a welcoming committee who greeted each of us as we left the boat. Men in colorful shirts and white pants stood off to the side, offering rides into town. The walkway wound past several eateries and bars, and the farther we went, the fewer people remained in our group. Ahead, the white beach beckoned. A couple of workers were lining up gold cane chairs like the ones from the Nautilus Shell onto the beach, and screens covered in tropical flowers set off the patch of beach where the group wedding was to take place. To the left of that zoned-off area was an outdoor cantina where a female bartender in a cropped tank top and long braids blended and served colorful island drinks.

"Which way?" I asked.

"You pick."

"It seems almost criminal to be this close to a beach and not experience it." I slipped off my sneakers and placed them into a plastic bag I'd packed for such an occasion. I put the bag into my handbag and stepped onto the white sand, wiggling my toes to feel the microparticles against my skin. It felt like I was standing in warm sugar.

Tex took off his sneakers and dangled them from his fingertips. He cuffed his trousers and joined me on the beach.

A Mexican man in blue approached us and held out a flyer. "Hola! Come join us at the Cozumel Cantina. One-dollar beers! Two-dollar island drinks! All are welcome!" He flashed us a blindingly white smile and moved on to distribute his adverts to the people behind us.

"Come on. I'll buy you a beer, and you can stop pretending you didn't notice the woman blending the drinks. Even I can tell there's something about her that's hard to ignore."

"You know I only have eyes for you."

We were back to our playful interaction. When I pushed the thoughts of danger out of my mind, it felt like we were one unit, seeing the same things and reading each other's thoughts. Not having the unique problems of our separate lives present in the immediate background made our unexpected harmony more evident. I wouldn't miss the threat of danger when we got back to Texas, but I would miss *this*.

We strode toward the cantina and took two seats by the bar. The bartender had her back to us. I got hit with an overwhelming sense of familiarity even though I'd never been to Mexico before. I pulled off my sunglasses and cleaned the lenses with the hem of my dress then put them back on and looked up—into the eyes of the woman who had orchestrated the entire getaway.

Nasty was on the beach.

CHAPTER TWENTY-FOUR

"Hola," Donna Nast said. Her name tag said Donita. Her face was completely impassive, as if her being there on that beach, offering to serve us strawberry margaritas while her hair swung behind her head in a multitude of braids tied off with plastic beads, was the most normal thing in the world.

I had a moment when I doubted it was her.

"Hola, Donita. Cómo estás?" Tex asked.

Nasty set a bowl of plantain chips in front of us. Tex took a handful and tossed them into his mouth. She didn't answer his question. She wiped her hands on a towel that was tucked into the waistband of her cut-off short shorts. Two young men pulled up the stools across from us and fist-bumped over their view of Nasty's butt.

"Yo soy… confused," I said.

"Let me recommend the margaritas," Nasty said.

"Sure. He'll have a—"

"Margarita," Tex said.

"You've been craving a Lone Star since we boarded the boat. What changed?"

"I'm on vacation," he told me. He shifted his attention from me to Nasty. "I hear people do all sorts of unusual things when they come to the islands."

Nasty, to her credit, kept her thoughts to herself. She left us sitting at the bar and blended two margaritas then returned before setting them in front of each of us. "How's your vacation so far?"

Tex pulled his drink closer and took a swig of it, leaving it up to me to interpret the question and provide an answer. I spun my drink—a plastic goblet with a thick, bright neon-pink base—in a circle of pooled condensation and stared at Nasty. I was twice her age and in terms of appearance darn close to her polar opposite, but along the way, I'd come to appreciate her intellect and skill set immeasurably. She'd come to trust me on occasion, and if I could rewrite any one detail from the past few weeks, it would have been that, that Nasty hadn't kept me in the dark about our assignment. I would have liked to know the truth from the beginning.

"We had an unusual first day," I said, maintaining eye contact. "There appeared to have been some sort of disagreement on the lido deck, and the purser—a man named Homer—ended up on the losing side of the argument."

Nasty's hands were wrist-deep in a sudsy plastic bin behind the bar, keeping herself busy with the tasks of a bartender working an open cantina on a beach. If I hadn't been looking for it, I might have missed her brief pause. All movement stopped, and her face clouded, or maybe it was a shadow from a passing biplane that pulled a banner announcing Happy Hour at Senior Frog's.

"What happened?" she asked.

Tex fielded that one. "Knife in the chest," he said right before taking another swig from his drink.

Nasty pulled her hands out of the water. Her hands were red, the color ending in a precise line above her wrist. It looked as if she was wearing gloves. She pulled the towel out from her waistband and wiped off her hands.

"Hey, Donita!" One of the guys who'd been ogling Nasty's rear view slapped the top of the wooden bar. "Can my buddy and I get a couple more beers?"

"Sure." She tossed her towel over her shoulder and pulled four Coronas out of a cooler, set them in a metal bucket, then filled the bucket with ice. She set the bucket on the counter in front of the guys. "Four dollars."

He set a five on the counter but kept his fingertips on the corner of the bill. "I'll make it ten if you agree to join us when your shift gets off."

She slid the bill out from under the guy's fingertips and tucked it into her macrame bikini top under her tank top. "Nah, five will do."

Another bartender, this one male, came over to Nasty. "You want a break?"

Nasty nodded. She turned and beckoned us to follow her. The bros seemed stunned. "She's going with them?" one asked.

"Dude, they probably tipped her a twenty."

Tex and I carried our drinks to a table on the beach. We were about twenty feet away from the cantina. On the opposite side of us, a crew adjusted the chairs for the beach wedding. The sun was bright overhead, and the surrounding sounds were a mixture of laughter and seagulls. I could see the promise of a vacation in Cozumel and made a mental note to come back. It seemed like nothing bad could happen here.

"Homer's dead," Tex said. "We recovered the stolen loot but don't have a suspect. Seems someone's onto Madison." He took another swig.

I pulled his drink closer to me. "What's in there, truth serum?"

"You should try it."

I pushed his drink back and turned to Nasty. "We have a list of suspects. Jennifer, the dive instructor. She doubles as a mermaid, and she was in the water near us when I found Homer's body. She could have stabbed him and dived overboard to have an alibi."

"It's not Jennifer," Tex said. He took another swig. "It could be Persephone. She's the decorator on the ship. She thinks Madison is cheating on me, and she's sympathetic to my cause."

Nasty raised her eyebrows.

I added, "She was in charge of setting up the stage for my performance last night, but the stereo system was rigged to blow when I pressed Play on the prerecorded tracks. She could easily have sabotaged it, knowing what would happen."

"Motive?"

"I think she and Homer were involved." I thought back to that early conversation to remember her exact words. "It's not what she said. It's what she didn't. She told me he volunteered to help her when they were..." I paused. "She didn't finish that thought. Her face flushed, and she said she should have thought about her job before..." I paused again. "She didn't finish that thought either."

"Circumstantial, but it sounds like there might be something there. Who else?"

"Those two women," Tex said. Either the alcohol was catching up to him, or he was purposely being vague.

"The Stork sisters?"

He nodded. When he didn't add elaborate, I did. "There are two sisters on the cruise. They're major Doris Day fans."

"As major as you?"

"Nobody's as big a Doris Day fan as Madison."

"There are Facebook groups that would beg to differ," I said.

"Tell me about these women," Nasty said.

I considered where to start. "Their names are Meg and Mavis Stork. Mid-sixties, I'd guess, Black women who dress in pastels. So far, they're the only two people who appear to want to be on this nostalgia cruise. They treat me like I'm a celebrity, and for a little bit, they tried to get me to go by Doris Day instead of Madison Templeton. I caught them both in lies, and I'm pretty sure they would alibi each other if they had to."

"What were these lies?"

"Mavis said Meg always spent the first day of a cruise in the room, resting and getting acclimated for the rest of the trip, but later, I found Mavis up and out, and she said Meg was the one resting in her room. I found both of them in the hallway near our original room, where we left Homer's body, which is the same hallway where our luggage was stashed. They had the opportunity to put the stolen loot in our suitcase when nobody else was around."

"Anything else?"

"They were at Madison's performance last night when the stereo system blew," Tex said. "And they were also on the previous cruise when the burglary took place."

"Sounds fishy," Nasty said. "You think maybe they're

kissing up to you because they suspect you of not being who you say?"

Tex and I glanced at each other. "They think Tex is a Russian cosmonaut named Vladimir Komarov," I said. "They encouraged me to have a fling with him while I'm on the ship."

"Have they met Mr. Templeton?" she asked with a quick glance at Tex.

"No, but they know he's also my manager, and that didn't work out too well for Doris Day."

"Could be they're onto you. Be careful around them."

I had a sudden vision of the Stork sisters in their elastic-waist pants, threatening Homer with a knife on the lido deck. The image seemed like something that would come out of a diverse edition of *Clue*, with a Filipino victim and an international backdrop. I didn't want to believe it, but I couldn't write off the possibility either. Even the bestseller lists spoke of an emerging trend toward late-in-life killers.

"Lenny, the boatswain, was first on the scene after us. He could have been waiting nearby after committing the crime for someone to discover the body. So far, he's the only one who knows we know Homer is dead. We helped him put in our original room, and he's the one who brought our luggage to our new quarters. He could have easily stashed the stolen loot in my suitcase."

"Plus he has a passkey," Tex added.

"*Had* a passkey," I clarified. "He loaned it to us for a little bit, but yes, he has a key that will unlock any room on the ship. That's access with a capital *A*."

"Theory?" Nasty asked. She tended to tip her head and sweep her long, copper-streaked hair over one shoulder, a gesture I'd watched her make over the years I'd known her.

Even her little boy grabbing handfuls of her hair hadn't broken her of the habit. She must have forgotten about her braids because now she did the gesture almost unconsciously. When her hand came into contact with the braids, she seemed surprised by the texture of her hair. If anybody in the area already knew Nasty, that one gesture would be what gave her away. I reached across the table and grabbed her wrist.

"Hold still." I stood up and went behind her, pulled her braids to the back of her head, and wove them in a thick braid down her back. There was nothing available to secure the bottom of the braid, so it was just a matter of time before it unraveled, but it would temporarily keep her from acting like herself.

While I stood behind Nasty, a man in a white guayabera shirt and loose white trousers approached us. "Hola, amigos! Are you coming to the wedding?"

"We're already married," Tex said. He held up his hand to show off his gold wedding band. I did too—and that was when I realized mine was missing.

CHAPTER TWENTY-FIVE

"It's gone," I exclaimed. I put my right hand over my left and massaged my ring finger with my thumb and forefinger. Wearing that solid band of gold had felt unfamiliar, and I'd caught myself worrying the soft metal from time to time since we'd departed. I must not have noticed when it fell off.

"Qué pasa?" called the bartender who had relieved Nasty at the cantina.

"No hay problema," Nasty called back. She turned and looked at me. "Take it down a notch."

I kept my hands balled together and glanced at Tex. The man in the guayabera stood near us with a concerned look on his face. "Estás bien?" he asked nervously.

"Sí," Nasty said.

The man nodded and moved on to a group of people sunning themselves on the beach.

"My ring is gone," I said, this time in a near whisper. "I don't know when I last had it."

"Nasty told you your rings would get loose," Tex said. He

took the final swig of his margarita, finishing with the sound of air being sucked up his straw. "Are you going to drink that?" He pointed at my drink.

I pushed the tall glass toward him. "I suppose it could have fallen off. I'm not used to wearing a wedding ring, so I might not have noticed it was gone, but if there's a thief on board the ship, it's just as likely that someone stole it."

"When did you last have it?"

I tried to remember where I'd been and whom I'd encountered. I had shaken a few hands along the way: Lenny, Jennifer, Willow, and two of the Tossed Pebbles. Then there was the pool when I lobbed the inflatable ball into the water. If my ring had been loose at the time, it could have slipped off then. Or backstage after my thwarted performance or even during the brief interlude Tex and I had spent in the bedroom of the Sanctuary. It could even have fallen off that first day when I found Homer's body.

"It could be anywhere." I glanced at Tex. "I'm sorry. I thought I was doing a good job protecting our cover, but I might have left evidence behind at a crime scene."

Tex slung his arm around my shoulders and pulled me close. "It'll turn up."

I started to make a comment about Island Tex, how this was yet another facet of his personality that I never could have predicted, when I spotted a crowd heading toward the wedding area. Several women were dressed in white, some in long, loose, flowy dresses, one in a caftan, and one in a strapless minidress. A stocky Mexican woman stood with a basket of flowers. She handed petite bouquets to each of the women who passed. I recognized the two couples who had been in the pool yesterday plus a few other people who seemed vaguely familiar. A lot of them had passed by me on the day the boat left Galveston, when I'd mingled with the passengers.

The crowd was largely festive—or drunk. A trio of musicians strolled behind the crowd, laying a soundtrack over the seagulls and laughter. An awful lot of people depleted their savings accounts for extravagant weddings, but this seemed special too. It would be easy for them to remember the day.

Nasty leaned in and spoke in a hushed voice. "Nobody reported a death on the ship. That's suspicious. Back at Big Bro, I had Bruce run background checks on the crew, but I'll see what we can find out about the Stork sisters." She looked at Tex. "I'll get Captain Komarov added to the passenger list so your cover—both of your covers—will be safe. Madison, you're going to have to lean into that. If Meg or Mavis or any of the passengers are the ones behind the thefts or the murder, the worst thing that can happen is for them to suspect you're not who or what you seem. I know this is asking a lot, but you might want to double down on the helpless-female act. Make it look like there's no way you could handle yourself in a dangerous situation."

Nasty's coworker beckoned to her, and she nodded at him. "I've got to get back to the cantina. After the ceremony, there's going to be a whole crowd over here. Keep an eye out for anybody who looks suspicious. I'll do the same."

I glanced over each shoulder. Tex finished my margarita.

"Do you know what you have to do?" I asked him.

He stopped slurping from the straw long enough to say, "I do."

Nasty left us alone at the table, and I took off my hat and tipped my face toward the sun. It felt good. If I remained like that for five minutes, I would have real freckles to go with the ones I painted on each morning. If I gave it fifteen minutes, I would be a lobster. But for a few seconds, I could enjoy the atmosphere, the peace, and the solitude.

A shadow fell over my face. I opened my eyes.

The male bartender was a few feet away. He held two fresh margaritas. "Who wants a refill?"

"I do," I said.

Tex shook his head. "I'm good."

"I should hope so," I said under my breath.

I raised the fresh drink to my lips and sipped tentatively. The sweet strawberry flavor was cut with tequila, providing a contrast of hot and cold as it trickled down my throat. My eyes widened.

"Take it easy with that," Tex said.

"Says the man who just polished off two in a row."

"Nasty made ours. No alcohol. They were a prop to make us look like we fit in."

I stared at the drink the bartender had handed me.

"Don't beat yourself up over it. You only had a sip. I'll get us a couple of beers." He leaned in and planted an unexpected kiss on my lips. He tasted like strawberries.

Tex left me at the table while he went to the cantina. I put my hat back over my head and turned my attention to the wedding ceremony. Couples were kissing in varying degrees of passion. All told, I counted seven different pairings. The oldest appeared to be in their seventies, and the youngest was the lead singer from the Tossed Pebbles with a woman I recognized from the cruise. I chuckled as I wondered if their marriage would last longer than Mick and Bianca's.

A group of women in bikini tops and frayed denim shorts ran past me. Tex trailed a few feet behind them with two bottles of Lone Star. He handed me one, and I tapped the neck of it against his in a toast.

"Enjoy it while it lasts," I said.

"Just protecting my cover like Nasty asked." He held out his hand. "Let's take a walk on the beach."

I took Tex's hand and stood. The fabric of my dress fell into place, loose around my legs. My handbag hung from the crook of my right elbow while I held my beer. Despite the murder, the theft, the frame-up, the pretend identities, the exploding stereo system, and the missing wedding ring, for the first time in a long time, I was at peace.

We strolled along the soft white beach. The sand had grown hotter under the glaring sun. The texture was soft and smooth, not grainy, and my feet sank in and left a trail of shallow footsteps to mark our path. The sun was no longer directly overhead. As long as people from our cruise were on the beach, we weren't at risk of being left behind.

Beyond the crowd was a shaded park furnished with empty net hammocks. Tex pulled me toward one. He took my beer and jammed both of our bottles into the sand next to the hammock then lay down and held out his hand. I climbed in next to him and nestled under his arm. He turned his head and pressed his lips against my temple, and I bent my arm and put my hand over his.

"This is nice," he said. "You and me. No case load, no administrative tasks, no meetings with the mayor to talk about budgets."

"No quarterly taxes, no loan payments, no house flippers looking to raze original mid-century properties," I said.

"No nephews."

I nodded at that one. The recent arrival of Tex's nephews

to Dallas had sidelined Tex in ways he never could have anticipated!

In the background, the trio of musicians started up with a new song. The melody emerged into a slow ballad. Tex swung his legs over his side of the hammock and stood, turned to me, and held out his hand. "Dance?"

"Here?"

"I won't tell anybody if you don't."

I took his hand and met him by the end of the hammock. He wrapped his arms around my waist. I put mine around his neck and rested my head against his collar. The music was faint, far enough away that only a few notes here and there stood out, but it was more than enough to create the atmosphere.

"You asked me why I checked your schedule back in Dallas. I wanted to surprise you with a getaway. These last few years have been a lot for both of us. Mickey and I got my boat up to code, and I can't think of another person I'd rather christen it with."

"A surprise getaway," I said. "That sounds nice."

"We could give it all up. My job, your business. We could sell everything we own, cash out, move to an island. You could wear a coconut bra and serve me bananas."

"Is that what you want?"

"I'm not opposed to the outfit."

I slapped him playfully. "You told me once that being a cop wasn't something you did, it was who you are. Do you think there's going to be a day, someday, when you walk away from it? When you stop being a detective?"

Tex didn't answer right away. I watched his profile as he looked up at the sky between the palm trees surrounding us.

"No. I don't think there's going to be a day when you stop being a decorator either."

"So we're going back. I guess there's no more bananas."

"Stick with me, and there will always be bananas." He put his right hand into the pocket of his trousers. "Hold out your left hand."

"Tex—"

"Do you trust me?"

"I do." I raised my left hand.

Tex pulled a gold band out of his pocket and slipped it onto my ring finger.

"Where did you find it?"

"Bathroom floor. Must have fallen off in the shower."

I held my hand up and spun the band in a circle with my thumb. It was nondescript, a simple gold band. Wedding rings were different from the other jewelry I acquired in my estate sale purchases. There was both a beauty and a sadness to finding them. It told me the deceased had dealt with loss when their partner died, that they'd finished out their life without their companion. It was easy to sell off the watches I found, but I kept the wedding rings because they symbolized something else. I would keep this one, too, for different reasons. A souvenir of sorts.

The last few years *had* been a lot. I'd seen the business end of more than one gun, and Tex had taken a few of the bullets intended for me. We'd started out as adversaries, and he'd become my best friend. My once-fledgling business was thriving, and he was the captain of the police force. Success felt great, but it also felt busy. The one commodity we'd both traded to get what we wanted was time.

We returned to the hammock. Tex kept one foot on the

ground and gently rocked us back and forth. Overhead, the blue sky peeked between the fronds of stately palm trees. If I were recreating the colors in a room, I would use Behr "Sun Valley" to capture the green, "Havana Coffee" for the trees, and—ignoring the cliché—"Paradise Sky" to capture the blue. In the past, I'd been tapped to endorse a collection of colors for a local paint store, and if I used the memory of today as inspiration for a new collection, I might call the trio of colors "Tex and Madison's Perfect Afternoon."

After a peaceful stretch of silence, I said, "You know, Captain, you're nothing like you seem."

Tex smiled. "I think the greater Dallas population of women between the ages of thirty-five and seventy would beg to differ."

"You have more crossover appeal than one of my targeted ads on social media."

"What can I say? I'm charming."

I might have stayed curled up under Tex's arm in the hammock for hours if we weren't being expected to do a job. Reluctantly, I shifted my weight and sat up. Tex stood and pulled our beer bottles out of the sand, and I dusted the residue from the bottom of my raffia handbag. I took his hand and followed him out of the clearing to the beach, where happy couples mingled with wedding spectators. At the back of the crowd stood the dive instructor, Jennifer, wearing a pink Lacoste shirt and white shorts. She wasn't wearing her wig, and her long red hair was pulled into a ponytail. I was about to call out to her when the Amazonian bride in the white caftan broke away from her dance partner and stormed toward Jennifer.

"Where did you get that?" she demanded. She grabbed Jennifer's wrist.

The pretty dive instructor yanked her arm back, but she wasn't fast enough or strong enough to break the bride's grip. The bride held Jennifer's wrist up over her head, and sunlight glinted against a delicate silver bracelet.

CHAPTER TWENTY-SIX

JENNIFER KEPT HER FIST BALLED UP BUT MADE NO MORE attempts to break free from the bride's hold.

"You broke into my room and stole that," the bride said. It was more an accusation than a question, a statement of fact that could have been true. Jennifer sure looked guilty.

Tex dropped my hand and raced forward. The soft sand slowed him down. I didn't bother trying to run; now that my knee felt stable, I didn't want to risk an awkward fall on the sand. I was curious about Tex's actions. Earlier, while we were recapping suspects to Nasty, he'd dismissed Jennifer as a possible suspect, and I wanted to know why.

"Break it up," Tex told the two women. He angled his body between them and pried the bride's fingers off Jennifer's arm. It was a testament to the bride's strength that a few beads of sweat appeared on Tex's forehead.

He turned his back to the bride and glared at Jennifer. "What's going on?"

"That's my bracelet," the bride said. "She stole it." She

reached over Tex's shoulder and grabbed at the air in front of Jennifer, trying to regain contact.

Jennifer backed away from Tex and put her hand on her wrist, covering the chain. Her eyes were wide with fear.

"She didn't steal that bracelet," Tex said. He turned to Jennifer. "Did you?"

"No," she said nervously. "It's mine."

"Then why does it have the initials RR engraved on the charm?"

Tex slowly reached forward and put his hand on Jennifer's arm. She balled up her fist but released the hand that covered the bracelet. Tex moved her arm toward him and inspected the bracelet.

It was a delicate silver chain with a rose-gold heart charm that was smaller than the nail on my pinky finger. Tex touched the small charm then moved the bracelet so the sun reflected off the surface. I leaned over Tex's shoulder and saw two letters engraved on it. They were cursive and appeared to have been hand drawn and not punched by a template. RR, just like the bride said.

"What's your name?" Tex asked the bride.

"Riva Ramirez."

I recognized the name. It corresponded to one of the names on the passenger manifest we had back in the room, the passengers who'd been divested of the personal belongings that had ended up in my suitcase.

No precious stones accented the bracelet, and no bling telegraphed its value to the world. If I had to guess, I would have said its worth was in nostalgia more than materials, which begged the question of why, if Jennifer was indeed behind the thefts in the staterooms, she had chosen to wear that particular item in public. Why flaunt something that could so easily be traced to someone that wasn't her?

"I'm sorry," she said. "I didn't know."

She unclipped the bracelet with her free hand and held it out to Riva, who put up both hands in a sign of refusal. "Oh no you don't. You're not getting off that easy. I'm turning you over to the authorities." She looked over her shoulder. "Lenny! Can you come over here?"

The four of us stood in an awkward cluster: Jennifer and Riva in a face-off, me and Tex between them. Since Riva had refused to take back her bracelet, Jennifer was left holding the hot item. We all knew it didn't belong to her, but nothing about the way she'd handled the accusation indicated a denial or a fight.

"I'll take that," I said. I relieved Jennifer of the bracelet and dropped it into my raffia handbag. I turned toward Riva. "I'm Madison. I'm staying in the Sanctuary. Come to my room later, and I'll make sure you get your bracelet back."

The bride's eyebrows were drawn together, two dark slashes made more emphatic with makeup. Her lips, a matte shade of red, pressed into an angry line. Not long ago, I'd watched her and the other brides head to the beach to exchange vows with their significant others, and I didn't think this incident was what she would want to remember today for. Once again, I found myself playing the mediator, slipping into the character of Doris Day to dissolve the tension of the encounter.

"You don't want to think about this today, do you? It's a glorious day on the beach, and it's the beginning of your life with your new spouse. I'm sure there's a perfect explanation for what happened, but don't let it get in the way of your celebration. Today's a new beginning."

The bride's expression changed, softening from anger to understanding. "You're right," she said. "Everything before today is in the past." In an unexpected impulsive gesture, she put her hand on mine and squeezed. "Thank you for the perspective. We brides have to stick together."

Before I could process what she meant, she glanced at Jennifer, her expression shifting toward disdain, then took the hand of a man a foot shorter than her and led him away.

Even though the tense situation had been defused, we hadn't completely shaken the attention of the crowd, and even though I'd had a hand in defusing the crowd, I couldn't deny that it looked bad for Jennifer. Tex had been so certain that she wasn't guilty, but she was right there with a piece of stolen jewelry, and she hadn't exactly denied the accusation of theft.

"I can explain," she said as if reading my thoughts.

"Maybe you should," I said.

Tex pointed at a nearby table and chairs. They were near enough to the entrance of the ship that to avoid being overheard, I lowered my voice.

"Where did you get that bracelet?"

"I found it."

"That's a pretty thin explanation," Tex said.

The accusations, the drama, the heat, or something else appeared to weigh on Jennifer. Her shoulders slanted downward, and her back curved. She kept her eyes on a knot on the wooden table instead of making eye contact with either one of us. She didn't look innocent, but her lack of fight made her appear to be something other than guilty. As if she wasn't entirely surprised by the accusation of theft.

"Where did you get it?" I asked again. That time, I made an effort to keep the judgment from my voice.

"It was stuck to my mermaid tail after a dive. I have three different costumes—an orange one, a turquoise one, and a pink one—and that day, I wore the orange one. When I return to the boat, the first thing I do is rinse out the costume and hang it in my shower to drip-dry. It's less damaging on the fabric, and those costumes don't come cheap."

I smiled to acknowledge that I believed at least one part of her story.

"Later that day, when I went to move the costume to my closet, I noticed something hanging from it. At first, I thought some of the gold trim had come loose, but it ended up being that bracelet. It must have snagged on the fabric. I took it to Homer. I thought maybe one of the guests dropped it and we should put it in lost and found. He said to keep it. He said people find things in the ocean all the time."

Aspects of Jennifer's story rang true, but there were red flags too. If she had indeed asked Homer, then was it coincidence that Homer was now dead? And what of the coincidence of getting a stolen piece of jewelry stuck to her mermaid tail on a trip sometime after the jewelry had been stolen? The whole story sounded suspicious, like it was designed to throw suspicion off her. Maybe she and Homer had been in on it together.

I glanced at Tex to gauge his reaction, but he was in cop mode. His face was a mask, hiding any reaction to the story Jennifer told us. It must have been off-putting, talking to a man who showed no response to her account of what had happened, so she played to the more understanding person at the table: me. But then again, Tex had been pretty sure that Jennifer wasn't guilty, and I still didn't know why.

Jennifer averted her eyes. She appeared to be

unburdening herself with us, but I sensed she hadn't told us the full truth.

"You're still hiding something," I said.

She looked up at me. "My wig," she said. "It's missing too. I wasn't going to say anything, but someone may be trying to make me look guilty of something."

"That's enough," Tex said.

I looked at him, my features probably in a similar arrangement as those of Riva before I'd talked her into dropping the matter. He jutted his chin behind me, and I turned. Willow approached us with two men in National Guard uniforms.

"Everything okay over here?" she asked.

I assessed the scene. We were on the landing outside of the ship. Most of the people waiting to get back onto the boat were gone, and only a few guests, posing for selfies a few feet from the ship's entrance, remained. Shifting my gaze, I scanned the landing, identifying a few more men in blue uniforms. As long as we stood on solid ground, we were in Mexico. Whatever it was Jennifer said she could explain, it would be better if the conversation took place on the *New Nautilus* than out here. I saw no reason to turn a stolen bracelet into an international incident.

"Everything's fine," I said, then I had an idea. "Would you take our picture?" I pulled my cell phone out of my handbag. I didn't have an internet connection, but the camera feature still worked. I woke up the screen and held the phone out to Willow. "For my scrapbook," I said.

The crew of the *New Nautilus* must have been used to taking people's pictures, because she took my phone and cued up the shot as if my request was one in a string of similar ones. Tex and I sandwiched Jennifer between us, and

I smiled my brightest smile. After a few awkward moments when I wasn't sure if Willow was done, she handed my phone back. I tapped the screen to put it to sleep and accidentally took another picture, a blurry snapshot of the first officer with the boat behind her.

"Jennifer, Lenny wants to see you," Willow said. "There are a few changes to the schedule for the return trip."

"I've got a tour group scheduled for the viewing booth in an hour."

"Not anymore. Go to the front of the line. He's waiting for you in the meeting room."

I glanced at Tex to see if he was thinking what I was. Jennifer was supposed to offer an explanation, but she was about to slip through our fingers. Tex didn't seem worried. A server approached with a tray of shelled oysters on a bed of ice, and Tex picked one up and tipped it to his lips. He looked for all the world like a man on vacation.

If Tex and I had any plans to keep Jennifer with us, they were dashed in that moment. Jennifer left us standing outside the entrance. I faced Tex, expecting him to go after her, but he didn't, and a moment later, she was gone.

"There's a reception at the pool," Willow said. "You can change if you want, but you don't have to."

"Was that on your schedule?" Tex asked me.

"I don't know," I replied. "Weren't you in charge of my schedule?"

Willow said, "The reception wasn't on your schedule. It's for couples who just got married. We never know who's going to participate in the group ceremony, so we leave the reception time blocked out on the schedule and make adjustments as needed. It's open to everybody, but the photographer gets there early to take the wedding portraits."

"I see. I would like to change into something more performance-ready."

Willow shook her head. "We have a stereo system hooked up for the reception. Nobody expects you to work. Not now."

I waved her off. "It's been such a perfect day I barely remember the equipment malfunction last night."

"Not that. I mean you get to celebrate your wedding like everybody else."

"What wedding?"

Willow looked troubled. She pointed over her shoulder with her thumb. "All those people on the beach were getting married. You guys didn't have to participate, but when I heard you both say 'I do,' I thought it was touching. I told the captain, and he agreed that after everything that's happened so far, you should get to enjoy the rest of the cruise as your honeymoon."

My arms were dangling by my sides, and the back of one hand brushed Tex's. He curled his hand around mine and held it tight. Any protestations that tried to bubble up out of my throat got suppressed by unspoken suspicions that this, too, was a ruse, that someone on the cruise wanted to keep Tex and me from finding out anything more than we already knew.

"We'll see you there," Tex said in a tight voice.

Willow left us on the landing. Neither Tex nor I moved an inch. We'd been in countless situations that neither one of us could have predicted, but it was starting to sound like we'd stumbled into the one set of circumstances that scared us both to death.

According to Willow, Tex and I had accidentally gotten married.

CHAPTER TWENTY-SEVEN

WE GOT ONTO THE BOAT AND MADE IT TO OUR ROOM IN silence. The easy camaraderie we'd had on the beach was gone, in its place a slew of unasked questions. It didn't seem possible that the wedding was real, but after such a romantic day on the beach, protesting our ill-conceived nuptials seemed like a buzzkill.

Besides, it couldn't be true.

Could it?

The door to our room clicked shut behind us. Tex held his finger up to his lips then did a walk-through, checking behind closet doors and curtains to make sure it was as we'd left it. He bent down by the bedroom entrance and tweaked an invisible thread that he'd stretched across the doorway.

"I don't think anybody's been in here," he said.

I waited until he removed the thread then entered the room and flopped onto the bed. "Did we just get married?"

"No." Tex turned around and pulled his Breitling cosmonaut watch out of a drawer. He snapped it over his wrist and turned back. "I don't think so. Do you?"

"No." I stood up and checked my reflection. "But I can see why they think we did."

"It might work for us."

"How?"

"Now you're off the hook for the rest of the cruise. You won't have to worry about performing anymore."

"Even that's suspicious. If someone wanted to out me as a double agent, they could have let me perform and make a fool of myself. But by sabotaging the stereo system, they did me a favor."

"Yes, but you lose access."

"You think that's what this is all about? Keeping us from having access?" A knock sounded on our door. "Is the captain going to make us move again?"

Tex put out his hand to keep me sitting on the bed. After he left the room, I stood and hovered by the door so I could overhear his conversation.

"Compliments of the captain," a male voice said, followed by the rattle of a cart.

I was curious enough that I poked my head out farther to see what we'd gotten. A bottle of champagne was nestled in a silver ice bucket next to a serving tray of lobster tails and lemon wedges. I didn't want to think about what this cruise was doing to my cholesterol levels. All I'd had to eat all day was a couple of plantain chips with half a beer, and I was ravenous. I stepped into the hallway just as the waiter handed Tex a folder.

"Here's the other thing you asked for."

I hung back, hiding most of my body behind the door, and watched Tex reach into his back pocket and pull out his wallet. He extracted a hundred-dollar bill and handed it to the waiter. "Thanks."

The waiter tucked the bill into the front pocket of his shirt, nodded, then turned and left.

Tex stuck the folder behind the microwave.

"I thought it was against company policy for the crew to accept tips," I said.

Tex jumped at my voice. "Jeez, Night. Don't sneak up on me like that. I thought I told you to wait in the bedroom."

"You were serious about that? What is this, 1959?"

He made a great act of scanning my daisy-appliqued dress.

"Oooooooh!" I exclaimed. I pushed past him and yanked the folder out from where he'd stashed it. When I opened it, pages fluttered out. There was a three-page credit report for one Homer Manalo, a series of photographs of a naked male body in a bathtub, and a medical report. I'd already seen the file Tex kept hidden in the cookie cabinet, but this was the kind of file a homicide detective might assemble while working a murder case.

I grabbed a fistful of papers and waved them in the air. "Is this what it looks like?"

"I can explain."

"You're investigating Homer's murder!"

"Of *course* I'm investigating Homer's murder."

"You said we were here to investigate the thefts! When you showed me the file Nasty gave you on Homer, I wanted to talk about his murder, and you very specifically said we weren't here to investigate a murder!"

"I know what I said."

"Then what's this?" I waved the file around again.

Tex leaned forward and snatched it from my hand. "I'm a homicide cop, Night. I only told you that to keep *you* from nosing around the murder."

"But we're here as a team. We're supposed to be working together."

"No, we're supposed to uncover a burglary ring together. The murder was never part of the deal. I told Nasty about Homer half an hour after it happened, and she wanted to cancel the whole thing. She was going to meet us in Cozumel and fly us back to Galveston. Too risky for us, too much possible blowback for her."

"You knew she was going to be on the beach?"

He nodded. "I didn't know you would braid each other's hair. That was a bonus."

"Ooooooooooh!"

On any other day, I would have laughed, but something felt different this time. Maybe it was a new lens through which to see our relationship, the fake marriage and the reality that it might always feel like this. That no matter how close we felt at times, there would always be times when secrets existed between us. Maybe time spent on a boat had altered my sense of perception. But I'd been here before, we both had, and today, I zagged instead of zigged.

"Are you never going to trust me?"

"This isn't about trust."

"Then what is it? This isn't the first time we've suspected different people in a case. The record shows that sometimes, I'm even right. Is there ever going to be a time when you share this part of your life with me?"

"This isn't a part of my life. It's what I do. There's a difference."

"That's not what you said on the beach. Your identity as a cop is you, and my identity as a decorator is me. Last week, I heard you carry on an entire conversation with your sister about sputnik lamps and bowtie sconces, so don't tell me I don't share details about my life with you."

"Those aren't details from your life, Night. Those are fixtures in a catalog."

"I don't know. I just don't know. This dance"—I moved my hand back and forth between us then pointed at the table and the file—"I don't know." I was frustrated by my inability to find the proper words to describe the utter frustration I felt. "To go from being as close as we were on the beach to as distant as we feel right now…it's jarring."

Tex slapped the folder on the table with a *smack*. We glared at each other across the table. "Have at it," he said.

My blood was boiling just enough that I almost said no, almost fell into his trap of giving me what I said I wanted simply to see if I would reject it out of anger.

But I didn't, not then, because the latch on the door clicked open, and the last person I expected to see walked in.

CHAPTER TWENTY-EIGHT

"You two need to knock it off," Nasty said. She closed the door behind her and leaned against it. "I can hear you arguing ten feet from your room." She picked up a bunch of grapes from a bowl of fruit and popped one into her mouth. She dropped the bunch and came over to the table before opening the folder and fanning the pages out.

"Where'd you get this?" she asked Tex.

"I texted photos to Imogene and had her loop in Lloyd."

"I thought Imogene was working on revisions to her mystery while watching Rocky at a hotel in Galveston," I said.

"She's watching Rocky at a hotel in Galveston but not working on revisions. That was a cover story."

"And Lloyd?"

"He's there too. They're dating."

Tex handed me his phone. I scrolled through a text change of crime scene photos, happy selfies of Imogene and Lloyd, with Rocky between them.

Lloyd was the medical examiner in Dallas. Tex frequently

relied on Lloyd's autopsy findings to uncover clues for a case. I imagined Imogene, the mystery writer, meeting Lloyd through her volunteer work at the precinct then getting to know him over coffee while she asked questions about his work for research. The relationship was convenient for Tex, who could text Imogene crime scene photos and ask Lloyd to study them and draw conclusions. None of it would be valid in an actual investigation, so I understood, without Tex spelling it out, that the situation was a house of cards built on favors and speculation. His investigation was unofficial, and Lloyd's findings were solely for the people in the room.

"What did Lloyd find?" Nasty asked.

Tex glanced at me, and I held his phone back out to him. "Go on, Captain. Bring us up to speed."

He set his phone on the table and pulled out a stack of slick photos out of his folder. They were pictures of Homer's body. I'd been the first one to see it, on the lido deck, with the knife in his chest, but I'd turned away and let Lenny and Tex cover him up and carry him to our original room. I'd retrieved ice cubes while they arranged him in the bathtub and had been in charge of the air conditioner while Lenny and Tex secured Homer's body. I hadn't spent a lot of time looking at or thinking about Homer from that point on other than him having been involved in the thefts we were here to investigate.

But faced with the photos, I found it impossible not to see the tragedy of his death. Homer had been an employee on the boat, someone who had been around long enough to work his way up the ranks through promotions and tenure. He'd been established as our contact, which meant someone had trusted him with the truth. But there he was, lifeless and in a bathtub, his shirt open to reveal a wound I didn't care to examine too closely. Tex had been right to keep these photos from me.

I turned away and put my hand over my mouth, fighting my suddenly roiling stomach.

"You okay, Madison?" Nasty asked.

I held up my hand to indicate I was fine. The last thing I needed was to look like I couldn't handle the exact thing I'd demanded moments ago.

When I turned back, Nasty and Tex were discussing the file. The photos of Homer were spread out, and from where I sat, I could see the bluish discoloration of his skin and the gash where the knife had stabbed him. I shifted my focus from the photos to the other file, the one Tex had already shown me when we first started discussing the case. It was right after the Roomba incident when Jennifer told me about Homer as the boatswain, how there'd been an accident and a woman slipped on the lido deck and fell off the boat. Homer had been the one to dive into the water and save her. I'd taken her story at face value.

"Why are you so sure Jennifer is innocent?" I asked.

Tex and Nasty looked up.

"Who's Jennifer?" Nasty asked.

"The dive instructor. She told me about the lawsuit against the *New Nautilus* that came out of Homer's negligence, and she was just caught wearing a piece of the stolen jewelry. She doubles as the ship mermaid and was in the water when we discovered Homer's body, so she could have stabbed him and then dived in to give herself an alibi."

"That does sound suspicious." Nasty looked at Tex.

"It's not Jennifer," he said again.

"Are you going to explain?" I asked.

I didn't bother pointing out again how Tex's radar had

failed him in the past, because his conviction was so solid that this didn't feel like blind faith in a suspect's proclamation of innocence. Tex knew something I didn't, and we were right back where we'd started.

We stared at each other while Nasty looked back and forth between our faces. Tex knew what I was thinking. The conversation about not sharing was too recent for him to have already forgotten.

"That's what I thought." I picked up my raffia handbag and my key card. "If I'm not needed here, I think I'll take a walk."

Tex didn't try to stop me.

I grabbed my sketch pad and left. I wasn't going to do anything foolish like confronting a suspect alone in the bowels of the ship. Even if I did think Tex knew something I didn't, I wasn't willing to write Jennifer off as a suspect just yet. I strolled down the carpeted aisle in the same direction I had the first night. Straight would take me to the staircase down to the glass bottom, right would take me up to the pools and the wedding reception. I didn't want to go to either by myself.

I went left, down the hall, toward the Nautilus Shell. Persephone wasn't my biggest fan, but since I'd been relieved of my performance duties, there was no rush for her to complete the room. I could work at my pace, take down the wall art, and reinstall it correctly, maybe even learn something about who had sabotaged the stereo system.

A thin strip of light trickled out from underneath the door of the Nautilus Shell. I tried the handle, and it gave under my grip. The room was empty. The art installation had been disassembled and lay in pieces, grouped randomly, on a tarp below the wall. The groupings had nothing to do with the way the installation was intended to go together, so I set my handbag down and lost myself in the new task of arranging them out as they would be installed.

The rest of the room had been cleared. The round tables were collapsed and leaned against a wall by the kitchen, and the gold cane chairs sat in stacks by the entrance. I walked over to them and discovered traces of sand on the carpet. These must have been the same chairs that had been set up for the beach wedding.

I didn't want to think about that. Not now. It was one thing to date Tex, but to marry him? Accidentally? Was that something I wanted?

It was just one of the many questions to come out of the trip, and the more I tried to push those questions from my mind, the more they pushed their way back in.

At home, when I was plagued with problems I wanted to ignore, I decorated. That was the reason I'd brought a sketchpad on the trip. The most effective thing for clearing my mind and allowing me to focus was to start with an empty room and imagine what it could be. To mentally sort through my inventory, choosing a pineapple lamp over a Nelson bubble lamp, weighing the option of stark lines over soft curves, or settling on a color palette that moved the concept along.

The problem with the whole boat was that the decorator viewed it as a tongue-in-cheek representation of what it could be. To me, a nostalgia cruise didn't have to be a joke. It was a chance to recreate a gorgeous design style while honoring the progress the world had made in every other way since the style was last popular.

Once the art installation was laid out properly, I carried my sketchpad backstage while I looked for a writing instrument. A pencil sat next to the sabotaged stereo system that had hijacked my performance.

Alone, with no one to tell me not to check it out, I set my sketchpad down and moved closer to the unit. The cord was unplugged, dangling alongside the receiver. A handwritten sign proclaiming the unit out of order had been taped to the top of it with the same blue quick-release painter's tape that had been used on the stage floor. I leaned forward to get a better look at the back of the unit and spotted a crumpled-up ball of paper sandwiched between the back of the unit and the wall.

I used the end of the pencil to poke at the paper until it came free, falling behind the table and to the ground. I got on the floor and crawled to the paper then smoothed it out against the abstract print on the carpet.

It was the ship's itinerary, a listing of every single activity that had taken place from the moment we first stepped foot onto the boat. A circle had been drawn around the listing for my performance, and the original time—eight o'clock—had been crossed off, with a five written next to it. It felt like it meant something, like whoever left that there had been keeping track of my schedule. But what was it still doing there? Why was it crumpled into a ball and wedged behind the system someone had rigged to blow? What did it have to do with Homer's murder or the thefts or anything else that had happened since the boat departed?

Just what I needed: more questions.

I flattened the sheet of paper and refolded it. I was about to pull myself up when I heard a female voice out front.

"Nobody's going to hear you. They're all at the party—including the singer. You wanted this chance, and you made it happen. It's now or never." And then a pause. "Who put this together?"

It was Persephone.

Slowly, I backed under the table and hid behind the tablecloth. My heart thumped in a beat that would have rivaled Gene Krupa. The tablecloth stilled, and I hugged my knees, happy I could comfortably sit in a position I rarely managed.

If anybody else had stumbled into the room and seen the organization of the art installation components on the tarp, they would have assumed Persephone had done it. She was the only person who knew she hadn't. I didn't know who was with her, but my interactions with her thus far hadn't been peaceful.

She had means, motive, and opportunity to each of the crimes that had been committed and she was here with me.

And nobody else knew where I was.

My desire to put distance between Tex and me had led me into another dangerous situation. And if he was right that Jennifer wasn't the killer, the position was wide open for Persephone. Suddenly, my need to be in the know felt a whole lot thinner.

I sat still and listened for sounds of Persephone—where she was, what she was doing, and why she was there. And a few moments after she first entered the room, she did the one thing that made her actions clear.

CHAPTER TWENTY-NINE

PERSEPHONE'S VOICE WAS STRONG AND VIBRANT. BY THE TIME she hit the words "just a little girl," I'd not only identified the lyrics of "Que Sera, Sera," but I recognized a whole different motivation for Persephone's animosity toward me: jealousy.

Persephone wasn't the best decorator on the boat, but she was the best singer (fake Mick Jagger notwithstanding).

I crawled out from under the table and stood. My white dress was rumpled, and I'd lost a daisy applique somewhere along the way, but that didn't matter anymore. I stood slightly behind the stage partition, still undetected, in a spot where I could watch Persephone perform to an imaginary audience out front.

She hadn't been talking to an accomplice; she'd been talking to herself.

Whereas I was so worried about singing songs I'd long since memorized that I arranged to have a recording of Doris Day to accompany me, Persephone needed no backup. Without any music, her voice was pitch perfect. I'd had a chance not too long ago to spend some time with a vocalist, and I understood that for Persephone to be able to sing like she did, she'd had that magical combination of talent and practice.

I let her finish the song before revealing myself with applause. She spun around so quickly she knocked the microphone stand over. It wasn't turned on—she didn't need any amplification, and besides, the stereo system didn't work—but she stood behind it, pretending, like a girl singing into her hairbrush. Color rose on her cheeks, turning her peachy complexion a ruddy shade.

"I thought I was alone," she said.

I strode out from behind the stage. "You're wonderful. You should have been on this stage, not me."

"I know," she said.

I hadn't expected that, but her next statement clarified a few things.

"Until this gig, I didn't know you could get fired from a job before it started."

"You're the original performer," I said, the already illuminated lightbulb over my head growing brighter. I thought back to the cover story Nasty, Tex, and I had brainstormed in Nasty's office that fateful day in Dallas. "They told me there was an issue with your paperwork." It was what Nasty told me to say if anybody asked how I got the job. "That's why they were so willing to hire me last minute. I look the part but lack the talent. I didn't know why that didn't matter more."

"Who told you there was an issue with my paperwork?" she asked, her eyes narrowing.

We were approaching delicate territory. Persephone no longer seemed to be a threat, but I'd been fooled by people in the past. I wasn't going to let down my guard just because I felt guilty for appropriating her job.

There was one way to protect my cover and keep things contained to the cover story. "Homer," I said. "He reached out to my manager, who made the rest of the arrangements."

Persephone climbed down from the stage and sat on the edge, dangling her ankles over the side. Her shoulders drooped. "Then he *did* want to cut all ties with me. I just wish he told me the truth instead of sticking me with this nightmare of a job."

I left my post at the side of the stage and joined her at its edge. "You two were a couple, weren't you?"

She glanced at me as if expecting a reprimand. I smiled warmly, hoping to encourage her by my lack of judgment.

"Homer and I were on again, off again. It's not easy to work with someone you're in a relationship with, especially in close quarters like a cruise. He knew everything about everybody, and when I first joined the company, he kept me in the loop. The attention made me feel special, at least until I heard the whispers about him."

"What whispers?"

"Cruise ships are like petri dishes when it comes to gossip. There were rumors about Homer, about other employees who no longer worked for the company, about how he got promoted after that accident where the woman fell off the boat. I asked him about it once, and he told me to drop it."

"Wasn't Homer qualified to be the entertainment director?"

"Sure he was. He worked for the *New Nautilus* for years. He started as a deckhand and then became the boatswain and finally the purser. He knew every inch of this boat and every detail of the schedule. He was great at his job. Some days, it felt like he was everywhere at once."

"If you thought he was qualified for the promotion, why did you ask him about it? I don't want to be insensitive, but it seems as if he thought you didn't believe in him."

"You misunderstood. I didn't ask him about how he got the promotion. I asked him about the accident. People said Homer knew the woman who fell. That her accident wasn't an accident but that he pushed her. Whatever he told the company was enough to close the lawsuit, but he wouldn't open that part of his life up to me, and as long as I knew he kept that secret, I felt like he probably kept other things from me too. I never got past that."

Wow. Accepting that would have been a big hurdle in any relationship.

I tried to picture being with someone who rejected my request to know about a part of his life, then the irony hit me. I was in a relationship just like that. How many times had I asked Tex to talk to me about his cases? How many times had I gotten information about one of his cases, told him what I knew, and gotten frustrated when he didn't automatically loop me into his official investigation?

But I understood why Tex didn't tell me those details. It might frustrate me but not in the way it once had. With his silence, Tex was trying to protect me. He was also protecting the life he knew, where he had the agency to go where he needed to go and do what he needed to do and not get distracted by what anybody might say about his actions.

Several years ago, when it seemed as if Tex and I were destined to head down paths that had intersected for only a brief moment, he'd told me I put a face on the people he'd sworn to protect. It had been a bittersweet conversation. In one moment in a cemetery in Dallas, Tex revealed more about himself than he had since I'd met him. It might have been the moment I first realized I was falling in love with him, though every one of my save-yourself alarms had kept me from taking that risk at the time.

The shock of seeing our relationship mirrored in the one described by Persephone was revealing. Time and time again, I'd let frustration over Tex's perceived secrets drive me to the point of frustration when those secrets weren't secrets at all. And after having possibly exchanged vows with me on a beach in Mexico, he was the one who accepted what we might have done, while I was the one who dug in the heels of her Keds and protested the outcome.

People liked to think they were good judges of character. We went through life meeting people and slotting them into boxes: friend, ally, potential romantic partner, threat. We made major, life-changing decisions based on little more than pheromones and chemistry. I'd been in too many life-threatening situations to still believe I was a good judge of character. Maybe none of us were. But I was too far into my life not to question how often I'd made the wrong judgment call. How often I expected someone to act in a professional manner, to have my best interests at heart. How often I'd done what felt right to me and put myself in danger. I wondered if life would be better if I started out suspicious, if every person I met got sorted into the don't-trust-them column until they proved their integrity. If I allowed only people who earned my trust into my life, how different would my life be?

Tex didn't keep secrets from me; he simply kept the dangerous aspects of his job from me. He'd told me once I wouldn't deserve the life he gave me, but he'd found a way to give me something different. Since then, he'd treated me like a partner, and I still acted as if he didn't. Captain Tex Allen wasn't the problem there. I was.

My heart swelled at the realization. I was lost in the moment, the realization that we *were* a team, that sometimes being a match meant we were on opposite sides of the equal sign, an equation that looked completely different from its other half but added up to the same thing.

Persephone mistook my extended silence for solidarity. "You might not think it's a big deal to keep secrets in a relationship, but I do."

It took me a moment to realize she still thought I was having an affair on the side. I'd been inside the Nautilus Shell when she led Tex here that first night, and it had seemed an awful lot to me like she was trying to give him a chance to have an affair of his own.

"You might have gotten the wrong impression about my husband and me. I'm very devoted to him."

"I heard about you and the cosmonaut."

"Who told you?"

"Does it matter? Word is out, Madison. I wouldn't expect you to understand how I feel, but in my world, you don't keep secrets from the person you love."

I wanted to protest, but the only explanation I had was that Tex and the cosmonaut were one and the same, and that was a secret I had sworn to keep. Persephone's relationship with Homer was probably nothing like mine with Tex. I was starting not see that few were.

"Homer might have had a noble reason for not telling you details. There might have been more to the story than anybody knew, and he might have wanted to protect you. He might have wanted to leave whatever happened behind, and he wanted you to be part of his future."

Persephone's lips were pursed, making her look pensive. She tore at her fingernails without seeming to know it, a universal nervous habit that made her seem anything but confident. I chose that moment to reveal myself.

"Back in Dallas, I'm a decorator. I specialize in the mid-century modern aesthetic. Your nightmare"—I gestured to the room—"is my dream." I picked up my sketchbook and handed it to her. "These are my ideas for decorating this ship, and I probably have most of the authentic fixtures in storage."

She flipped through the pages, pausing to read the notes, and ran her fingertip over the room renderings. "How does that qualify you to sing?"

I smiled. "It doesn't. But I *am* qualified to properly install that art thingy if you want."

Before she could accept my offer, Willow's voice came over the loudspeaker. "Welcome back, guests! We at the *New Nautilus* hope you had a fine time in Mexico. If you're one of our brides or grooms, join us on the mezzanine for a reception that promises to go until dawn. There's bottomless champagne, dancing, and a moonlight swim. If it's stargazing you want, the promenade deck is the perfect spot to find your place in the universe. Telescopes are being set up for a midnight viewing of the night sky, navigated by Homer, our in-house astronomer. Leave your phones in your room. This is a phone-free event. The viewing starts at eleven forty-five."

At the mention of Homer's name, I sat up. "That announcement! She just said Homer would be on the promenade deck."

Persephone nodded. A tear trickled down her cheek, and she swiped at it. "That was his favorite part of the trip. Being on the promenade deck on the final night of the cruise. For one hour, the navigator kills the exterior lights and uses autopilot so stargazers get the best view. It's an all-hands-on-deck event, though. You'd be surprised how many people show up in their party clothes after drinking too much booze at the pool."

"But she said *Homer*..."

She waved her hand dismissively. "Those announcements are recorded before the ship departs. They let the crew be in two places at once."

That was it. That was the key. Someone *had* been in two places at once, but it wasn't Homer.

I wanted to run out of the room, to find Tex and tell him I'd been wrong—we'd *both* been wrong. I wanted to revisit the evidence and come up with a new conclusion based on that information, but I couldn't just leave Persephone alone.

Actually, I could.

And I might not know where everybody else on the boat would be, but after hearing that announcement, I knew exactly where to find the ship's resident spaceman.

CHAPTER THIRTY

"I NEED TO LEAVE," I SAID. "MY HUSBAND AND I RENEWED OUR vows while in Cozumel. We made plans to meet on the promenade deck at midnight."

Persephone looked up at me. "You did?"

"I told you, you're wrong about us. We're a team. Where he goes, I go." I pointed at the clock at the back of the room. It was eleven forty. "And right now, I'm going to look at the stars. Are you going to be okay?"

"Sure," she said, "but you don't have to rush. There's nobody to step in for Homer, so it's just going to be a bunch of people standing around a bunch of telescopes. Besides, all the clocks on the boat are twenty minutes fast, so if you leave now, you're going to be early."

I froze. Every person on the boat had been told to leave their watches in the room. Events were deemed to be phone-free. Clocks posted around the ship indicated the time. But if the clocks were all fast, then the timeline we'd all accepted was not set in stone. Time on the boat was as fluid as the ocean.

Twenty minutes was all it would take to get away with murder.

I felt like a vessel overflowing with facts that altered everything. I had to get out of there—I had to find Tex before he let his blind spot lead him into a vulnerable situation.

After leaving Persephone with my best wishes for her singing aspirations and a phoned-in sentiment about things working out for the best, I burst into the hallway. Unlike earlier, I wasn't alone. Couples in festive party attire stumbled toward me. I recognized Mick Jagger with his exotic bride, followed by Ronnie Wood, Keith Richards, and Charlie Watts. The women who'd been batting around the beach ball in the pool trailed them. Mick held a bottle of champagne by the neck, and Keith had his arm hooked around the brunette's shoulders. He planted a sloppy kiss on her lips, and they fell into the wall then bounced off as if it was made of rubber.

"Hello, love," Ronnie said in a passable West London accent.

The two women giggled. Keith draped his free arm around the blonde. People did get into the act, didn't they?

"Fancy joining us for a party?"

"She's Doris Day," Keith said. "She's not free to party."

"Don't be so sure," I said. "I'm free to do what I want any old time." I pushed past them to the sounds of "good one" and "she got you, mate."

Right before I rounded the corner, Keith called out, "Hey, Doris!"

I turned back, impatient.

"You can't always get what you want," he called out. He seemed proud of the comeback even if it had taken him a little too long to come up with it.

"I wouldn't be so sure of that either."

The Tossed Pebbles were just the beginning of a procession of party people in the hallways, and I navigated a labyrinth of good times on my way to the promenade deck. Details that I'd picked up during the whole trip were fitting together in a pattern that slowly revealed itself.

The promenade deck at midnight, with the lights on the boat turned off. It would be the perfect opportunity to rob people, especially if they arrived drunk and in their party finest. I imagined the cruise ship burglar working the crowd, easily unclasping necklaces and bracelets, maybe removing a watch or two from people who passed out. If I hadn't experienced the free-flowing booze of the cruise firsthand, I might not have believed it, but after having participated for two days, I could say with very little doubt that the trip wasn't about nostalgia but about having a safe space to get toasted. Even the two men who'd complained about their girlfriends dragging them along on the cruise had gotten over the novelty and joined in the fun.

I was getting a picture of what might have happened. Someone robbed people on the boat under the cloak of midnight while Homer conducted a tour of the stars. Whether he knew about the crimes as they happened or had discovered them after the fact didn't matter. Maybe he'd tried to stop the burglar. Maybe he'd demanded a cut. Either way, he had threatened someone's criminal enterprise, and that had gotten him killed.

But nobody knew that. The announcement led unsuspecting people to an event where the circumstances would be perfect for perpetrating a crime. If someone on the boat was the thief, then this might be his or her last time to get away with a fresh haul. The stash of stolen property in my suitcase would be the perfect diversion; Galveston police would be so tied up processing the valuables and reporting the recovery to the insurance company that the thief would walk through customs with immunity.

I didn't have much of a strategy, but I did know there was safety in numbers. It was the same notion Tex had conveyed when he first drew his map. If I thought I was in danger, I should go to the pool, where there was a crowd. Right then, the crowd was headed in the same direction I was, though I couldn't shake the fact that none of us were safe. Nasty was somewhere on the boat, likely with Tex, and when I found them, there would be three of us. Other than that, my plan was murky.

I was certain Tex would have heard that announcement and figured out the same thing I had. Three sets of eyes were better than two, and two were better than one. Tex was right when he reminded me that we were there to expose a burglary ring, not a murderer. Eyes on the prize.

The closer I got to the promenade deck, the slower my progress. The cruise accommodated four hundred guests, but according to the staff, it was only halfway booked. That meant there were two hundred people aboard, and I'd interacted with only a handful of them. I spotted a woman I hadn't yet met in a crew uniform at the end of the doorway, holding the entrance open while people filtered through and ascended a short staircase that led up.

The stairway was illuminated by a band of lights on either side of the stair treads. As I reached the stairwell, I saw what slowed down the crowd.

"No phones or flashlights allowed past this spot," the crew member instructed. "We need complete darkness for stargazing." She had a box of black pouches that she distributed to the crowd. People slipped their phones inside the pouches then handed them to her in exchange for a plastic token that identified their pouch. She attached a matching token to each pouch, not unlike a coat check. The woman smiled at me and waved me to the front of the line.

"Phone?"

"I didn't bring one," I said.

"Then you can head on up."

I held the fabric of my skirt close to my legs as I climbed the stairs. This wasn't the most practical outfit that I could have worn, but as I looked around at my fellow stargazers, I realized nobody here was dressed practically, and that was likely the point. I was more certain than ever that the crime I'd been brought on board to investigate was about to be committed again. I searched the meager crowd, but the lack of lights made it difficult to distinguish familiar faces—which did not work in reverse. When I felt a tap on my shoulder, I turned and found myself face-to-face with Meg and Mavis.

Unlike most of the passengers, the sisters had not opted for fancy attire for the evening. Meg sported a white T-shirt that pictured a kitten dressed as Sherlock Holmes, and she wore it under a pink-and-white gingham shirt with three-quarter-length sleeves and pink capri pants. Mavis wore an aqua zip-front hoodie and white pants. Her earrings were tiny lifesavers—the flotation device, not the candy.

"My sister said she saw you on the beach with that hunky cosmonaut." Meg waggled her eyebrows up and down at me. "I'd like to ride his rocket."

It wasn't what I expected to hear from a woman in a kitten T-shirt.

"You're so bad," Mavis said to her sister.

"What? It's not every day you meet a man who went to space. Madison knows. That's why she turned her back on her husband."

"It's just as well," Meg said. "He's been running around with that dive instructor as if nobody noticed." She thumped her chest. "*I* noticed. He doesn't deserve you, Madison."

"When did you meet my husband?" I asked nervously.

"I didn't, not exactly. I went down to the observation deck to arrange a dive with Jennifer, and she told me she was in the middle of a private lesson with Mr. Templeton. I spent the next six hours trying to track down the purser to arrange some private lessons of my own. Talk about the runaround. The boatswain finally told me there *are* no private lessons." Meg placed her hand on my wrist. "I'm sorry, Madison. Tex Templeton isn't the man you think he is."

Alarm bells rang in my head. I didn't know what Tex had been doing with Jennifer, but he'd been so certain of her innocence that he must have known something I didn't. But if he showed up there on the promenade deck, he wouldn't know whether to be Tex Templeton or Captain Komarov, and one false step would give him away.

I faked a smile and patted Meg's hand. "Relationships aren't easy. Sometimes we think we know someone, and they surprise us by showing us a side we never could have imagined." I pulled my hand away from her and took a step backward. "Would you excuse me? I don't think I'm up for this tonight."

"Of course." The sisters shared a look of pity at my dire romantic circumstances.

Once again, I found myself thinking every person I met was a possible burglar or murderer. Here I was, face to face with two people who had landed on Tex and my suspect list, and I was reminded of Tex's question asking if Meg and Mavis Stork seemed like real Doris Day fans or if they could be faking it.

"You never told me how you became fans of Doris Day," I said to them.

"Sly Stone," Mavis said. She clutched her hands together and swooned.

I studied her expression. It was hard to believe, but there *had* been a time when Doris Day was romantically linked to Sly Stone. "Those were just rumors," I said tentatively.

Meg flapped her hand. "We never thought they dated. Sly denied that when he was on Letterman, and honestly, I never could see them together. She means Sly and the Family Stone."

I searched for the obscure piece of trivia that connected the two, and then it came to me. "Que Sera, Sera?"

"Yes!"

In the early seventies, Sly and the Family Stone recorded a cover of "Que Sera Sera," and it became a hit. The choice sparked tabloid gossip that Sly and Doris—the kind of pairing that would sell copies—were a couple, though the rumor had never been substantiated. Over a decade later, the song played over the closing credits to the movie *Heathers*, giving it an even broader audience.

Mavis grinned widely. "When I heard Sly and the Family Stone sing that song, I knew I'd heard it before, but I didn't know where. I found out it was originally sung by this white lady named Doris Day, and when I heard her voice, it knocked me out."

There were a lot of ways to come to Doris Day. Mine came from being born on her birthday and watching her movies with my parents before they died. Some came to her through a love of Hitchcock movies, and some came to her through her animal rights activism. Meg and Mavis coming to her through a cover of Doris's signature song didn't surprise me one bit, and it convinced me of one major point: the sisters weren't faking their fandom.

A sense of calm settled onto my shoulders. For the first time since this cruise had left the dock in Galveston, I felt as if I were talking to two women who were exactly who they said they were.

I was about to ask their favorite movie when the two men who had initially resisted the idea of the cruise approached to the left of Meg. The taller of the two nodded in my direction and raised his beer in a toast. "Congratulations. Tell Allen I owe him a bachelor party."

It took me a moment to realize the man said Tex's real name, a moment that lasted too long and led to an unfortunate clarification.

"I should have introduced myself earlier. I'm Sam Bogosian. I saw you with Captain Tex Allen on the beach, didn't I? He and I did time together at the police academy before I transferred to the Austin unit. I didn't say anything earlier because I thought he was working a case too."

"This is just a vacation for us," I said quickly while searching my memory for where I'd heard his name before. *Bogosian.* I knew that name. But from where? Something on the ship. Somewhere—

"Lucky him. Can't remember the last time I had one of those. Enjoy it."

The man strayed away from us. I glanced at the Storks, who no longer looked at me with pity—or appreciation.

"Captain Tex *Allen?*" Mavis asked. "I thought he was Captain Komarov."

"He's a cop?" Meg looked perplexed. "I thought he was a cosmonaut."

"I can explain," I said.

"No need," Mavis said while Meg nodded emphatically. "We don't have time for liars. You probably don't even like Doris Day."

"I wouldn't lie about that."

"Come on, Meg. Let's go find Ronnie Wood. At least *he* pretends to have an accent." The two women left in a huff that may or may not have been warranted.

I had to find Tex. Not just because his cover was blown but because there was something else. The name Sam Bogosian clicked. It was on the itinerary for the previous cruise. I'd spotted the name on the passenger manifest, and when I showed Tex, he'd reacted but tried to brush it off. He must have recognized the name at the time.

And Sam had asked if Tex was working a case *too*. The phone call I intercepted on the day of departure: *There's a cop on the boat.* That call wasn't about Tex. It was about *Sam*.

Little details lined up: the girlfriends who appeared to have more interest in the Tossed Pebbles than their boyfriends, the overblown annoyance the men had shown at being dragged onto the cruise. How those two men were never around when Tex was. Sam was protecting his cover just like Tex. We already knew people on the boat were not who they seemed, but that meant—or it could mean—that we had backup.

I didn't care that Tex didn't confide in me at the time, not anymore. If the chips fell my way, we would have a team of four.

The promenade deck had swelled with cruisers eager to view the stars. I pushed against them to leave. Where my arrival had been with the tide, my departure went against it, and it took more than "excuse me" to cut a path through the crowd. All the while, I recognized the faults in my plan to find Tex there, that night, among everybody else.

I'd made a gross miscalculation. Tex had a memory for faces, and he must have known there was a risk in being outed if he spent too much time among cruise guests. Tex may know Sam was on board, but he wouldn't take the chance of showing up anywhere else he could be recognized. And if he wasn't here, then he would be in our room.

I shouldered past Riva and her short groom. I spotted Nasty by the top of the stairs and threw an elbow into my efforts to part the crowd.

"Where is Tex?" I asked when I reached her.

"He didn't find you?"

"No, but he's in trouble. I think the thief is going to strike here tonight, but Tex's cover has been blown." I turned and pointed out the cop. "That guy went to the police academy with Tex. He's working a case here too. He recognized Tex and said something, but aside from the two Doris Day fans who thought he was a cosmonaut, I can't tell who else heard. I'm going back to our room to warn him. If you see him, send him there to meet me."

Without wasting time on a further explanation, I dashed down the stairs. I fought against the cluster of people in the hallway with a renewed sense of urgency until I broke free from the pack and made my way to the luxury suite. I pulled my key card out and wanded it by the door.

It didn't work. I rubbed the small plastic card against my hip and tried again, but the light blinked red. I wiped over the magnetic strip with my thumb and tried a third time. I pounded on the door and pressed my ear to it, but there were no sounds and no reply.

"Mrs. Templeton?" asked a voice behind me.

I turned and spotted Willow.

"Is everything okay?"

"No." I wiped the dampness off my forehead with the back of my arm. "My key card won't unlock my door, and I have to get inside." I glanced at the keys hanging around her neck. "Could you let me in? My husband isn't answering, and I'm afraid something might have happened to him."

"Is he sick?"

"His heart," I said without thinking. "You wouldn't know it to look at him, but it's given him problems his whole life."

Willow glanced both ways then wanded her passkey across the lock. The light switched to green, and the door released. I turned the handle and burst inside.

Clothes were strewn everywhere. All of our suitcases were open, and garment bags had been unzipped and tossed. Several of the dresses I'd packed for performances were on the floor, crumpled in colorful piles of sequins and chiffon on the unimaginative carpet. The sliding doors were open, and the curtains blew inside along with the same crisp ocean breeze I'd found so pleasant when we arrived.

I dashed across the room and looked to the left and the right—and down at the water's surface, though I hoped I would not see anything or anyone there—but there were no signs of Tex.

I walked over to my suitcase and flipped it open. The stolen jewelry was gone.

"Where did you put it?" Willow asked behind me.

I should have known from the question that I'd walked right into a trap.

CHAPTER THIRTY-ONE

Willow stood just inside the bedroom doorway with a small knife in her hand. Her elbow was bent, and her arm was tucked against her side. She seemed perfectly comfortable with her weapon, and that scared me more than the weapon itself.

Actually, it might have been a draw.

"I don't know where the jewelry went." I glanced at the costumes on the floor. "Did you do this? Break in and toss my room?"

I meant it as an accusation, but Willow interpreted the question differently. "You didn't leave it like this?"

"With my costumes strewn around the room? No, this is not how I live."

"Someone else was here." Her eyes darted around the room, looking wild, seeking evidence to back up her conclusion. "Somebody else knows what I did."

We were across the room from each other, and even though Willow was distracted just enough to have let the knife point toward the bed between us and not at me, I wasn't confident that I could rush her before she snapped back to attention.

The way things stood, I was in trouble. My plan to find my people, to stick together, was blown. Nasty was on the promenade deck with a crowd. She'd thought she had a chance to catch the thief, and that was her goal. I'd believed the same thing until about three and a half minutes ago. Nasty had no way of knowing the thief was here, in my room, more interested in the stolen merchandise that no one else knew about than the possibility of a second heist.

It didn't take long to recognize a dire situation, especially when you were on a boat after midnight and the only available exit led to the ocean. Taking a swan dive into the choppy waters seemed as dangerous as facing Willow and her knife.

As Willow literally backed me into a corner, I tried to view the room differently. Instead of looking at lamps and furniture and curtains and an unimaginative decorating style, I looked for something to use to defend myself. But I was in the worst possible spot, on my side of the bed, with a wall-mounted light fixture and a nightstand.

The nightstand. The drawer.

I'd watched Tex slide open his nightstand drawer. I'd watched the drawer come free with a very small tug, somewhere between our morning move-in and our afternoon delight. I was nowhere close to the room's exit, but I was a foot away from my nightstand drawer, and if something—anything—would distract Willow for even a moment, I had a chance of pulling out that drawer and using it to defend myself. It was that or nothing.

The problem was finding a distraction.

I inched toward the nightstand. I thought my movement

was subtle, but Willow snapped to attention and drew the knife up into a defensive position.

"Relax, Madison. I don't want to kill you. Too much mess." She twisted her wrist. "But a knife wound should be just enough to get you to bleed out in the ocean. Maybe attract a few friends while you're out there." She gestured toward the sliding doors. "If you're lucky, someone from the boat will spot you after you fall overboard. Jennifer fancies herself a rescuer. It *is* a shame that it's the middle of the night. It took this cruise two hours to pull me up when I fell overboard, but there's a possibility that they won't notice you're missing until it's too late."

My heart thumped so loudly I could barely hear, but the word "overboard" tripped a wire in my memory. "You're the woman who fell off the boat because of the Roomba. The boat anchored to save your life."

"That's how they see it."

"You're lucky to be alive."

"That accident cost me a sweet payday. My fence was waiting for me in Cozumel, but that accident put us behind schedule. I missed our meetup. Now I've got some very dangerous men waiting for me to deliver. I was stuck on the boat with a suitcase full of stolen goods that were going to be discovered the minute one of these privileged passengers reported their valuables missing."

"Homer knew this boat better than anybody. He helped you hide the stolen property on the cruise, didn't he?"

She glared at me. "You know more than I thought."

"It's true, isn't it? Homer was your partner. But you didn't want a partner, so you killed him."

As I lobbed accusations at her, I repositioned my feet by the smallest amount, what felt like a centimeter at a time, closer and closer to the nightstand. The tip of Willow's knife glinted under the overhead lights, reflecting back at me.

She stepped closer, and I stepped back. The only place for me to go was out of the room, onto the balcony, and into the water. I maintained eye contact with her because staring at the knife did nothing to help me with my predicament.

"Yes, I killed Homer," she said. "He left me with no other options. He could have looked the other way. He didn't. He pressed me for a piece of the action. Said he'd open an investigation into my accident. The only way my plan worked was to get off the boat in Cozumel, fence the merch, and disappear. I could have returned to the States in a month or two or stayed in Mexico, where I was untouchable. Homer knew the longer he kept me on the boat, the more likely it was that I'd be caught."

"You planted that bracelet on Jennifer, didn't you?"

She shook her head. "The *New Nautilus* didn't hire Jennifer until later. Homer said we needed a scapegoat. He kept the bracelet and planted it on her mermaid costume the day she started. Insurance in case anybody started sniffing too closely."

"Why Jennifer?"

"He was sleeping with half the women on this boat, but she's the only one who ever rejected him. I guess that made her just special enough to frame."

I shifted my foot. My arms hung by my sides. I turned my hand out to see how close I was to the nightstand.

"What are you doing with your hand?" Willow demanded.

"My wrist cramped." I slowly raised my hands in front of me and balled up my left fist then rotated it in circles as if to prove my point. I held my left wrist in my right hand, selling my lie. My left leg grazed the corner of the nightstand, and I knew I was close enough, that it was now or never, that the next minute could go one of two ways, and only one of them was in my favor.

In a swift move, Willow rounded the corner of the bed and closed the distance between us. She pressed the tip of the knife into my throat.

"I should thank you," she said. "You or your scientist husband."

"He's not a scientist. He's a cop."

Willow blanched. Her eyes widened, and beads of perspiration dotted her hairline. She didn't appear to have suspected Tex was anything other than what she thought, and of all of his cruise identities, scientist was the strangest one to believe.

"Nice try." She stepped back and pulled a piece of paper out of her pocket. It was folded down to reveal the equal sign, the diagonal line up, the diagonal line down, the O and the X, and a few additional calculations. Tex's rudimentary map of the boat. It was signed *Komarov*. Those equations of his have to be worth more than a suitcase full of baubles."

I laughed. Of all the mix-ups that could have taken place while on the boat, all the cover stories and lies and pretend identities Tex and I had juggled, that one piece of trash had the potential to save my life.

At my unexpected outburst, Willow raised the knife. The door to the bathroom behind her slid open. We weren't alone. Willow turned toward the sound, and it was just enough time for me to bend down and yank the nightstand drawer free.

But I didn't need a weapon, because the element of surprise rendered Willow inactive. An imposing woman in a blond wig, pink caftan, and Revlon Moon Drops Apple

Polish lipstick stormed out of the restroom and put Willow in a full nelson.

I used the word "woman" loosely, because under the wig and the lipstick and the colorful caftan was the last person I expected to have borrowed my clothes.

CHAPTER THIRTY-TWO

Tex did not make an attractive woman.

The fabric of the caftan billowed around his torso. We locked eyes, and the adrenaline coursing through my body kept me from making any comments that might undermine the fact that Tex was exactly where I needed him to be when I needed him to be there. On a cruise where nobody was who they seemed, Tex was the most dependable person I could have conjured, and that was how it felt—that I'd conjured him by simply believing he and I would reach the same conclusion at the same time.

"Nightstand. Cuffs," Tex barked.

Willow struggled against Tex's hold, but she was no match for him. She twisted her torso and looked up at him. Then she saw what I did, but to her, it was no joke.

I circled the bed and dumped Tex's nightstand drawer onto the bed. A bundle of white plastic zip tie handcuffs fell to the center of the bedspread with the rest of Tex's personal belongings. I pulled one loose and held it out. Tex held her wrists together while I bound them and tightened the plastic.

I didn't have the same experience with zip tie handcuffs that Tex did, and by the time I finished, the plastic bit into her flesh. I didn't feel particularly guilty.

I did, however, feel grateful. So grateful that, despite the ridiculous costume Tex had donned to hide his true identity, I kissed him and smudged his lipstick.

I leaned back and straightened his wig. "Not bad," I said, "but I think you look better in blue."

* * *

WE WERE lucky to have a team in place after all. I located Nasty and asked her to find Sam Bogosian, the police officer who had blown Tex's cover. The two of them followed me to the Sanctuary where Tex babysat Willow. By the time we arrived, Tex looked like Tex again. It pleased me on a deep, emotionally intimate level that there would be one memory from the trip that existed between me and Tex and nobody else—except for Willow, who had bigger problems.

The mess in the room had been courtesy of Tex. Unbeknownst to me, he'd already considered the mounting possibilities of blowing his cover, and he knew if he were to leave the room to explore the ship, there was only one way to keep from being recognized as Tex Templeton, Vladimir Komarov, or Captain Tex Allen, and that was dressing up as, well, me.

After I returned to the room with reinforcements, Tex revealed what had happened to the stolen merchandise. He'd put it in the safe along with Homer's background check and autopsy photos.

I learned a few things after the fact. The phone call that I intercepted after Lenny placed Tex and I in room 307 was Willow.

Willow maintained her burglary was a victimless crime, but Homer's body begged to differ. The first matter of business after landing in Galveston was to turn Homer over to the Galveston medical examiner, who already had Lloyd's preliminary findings.

The second matter was to turn Willow over to the authorities. In addition to burglary, murder, and attempted murder, she faced charges of conspiracy to defraud an insurance company. Willow wasn't going to be cruising for a very long time.

But all of that had to wait until we docked.

Tex and I ignored the piles of clothes strewn around the room and crashed. Despite the bright sunlight streaming into our room, we slept until after eleven the following day. The room was a mess, but I didn't care about anything other than where I was and who I was with. It had been a long, strange journey, but somehow, we'd made it through, a team that operated independently but came together when needed. Not two halves but two wholes. It made sense that way. More than I'd originally thought.

The *New Nautilus* scrapped the original agenda for the final day of the cruise. Once word of the purser's murder on the lido deck leaked to the passengers, the idea of playing shuffleboard over the crime scene lost its luster. The insurance company, pleased that the stolen loot had been recovered, offered to reimburse the cost of the cruise for all passengers. It was small consolation to people like Meg and Mavis Stork, who had been there to enjoy the promise of a retro cruise with a fake Doris Day.

Who was I to disappoint them?

I shook out my performance costumes and packed them in their garment bags. I found a bellhop, borrowed a luggage cart, and loaded it with bags, then I asked for it to be delivered to Persephone with a personal note.

Please accept these costumes. They belong with someone who will wear them to perform. All best, Madison Night

Later that afternoon, Persephone took to the stage by the pool. The Tossed Pebbles joined her in a rendition of "The Glass Bottom Boat," and for two minutes and fifty-eight seconds, the crowd forgot about anything bad that had transpired on their trip.

The sun was bright overhead. I lay on a chaise next to Tex, slathered in sunscreen. I wore a vintage bathing suit with a yellow beach cover-up and a straw hat that cast a shadow over my face, neck, and shoulders. I was more relaxed than I'd been since departing thanks to my second mimosa.

I set my hat on my lap and turned to Tex, who was face down on the chaise next to me.

"I've been alone for a very long time. Even when I wasn't alone, I was alone."

Tex rolled onto his side and propped his head on his fist. "You're not alone, and you'll never be alone again. You're an inconvenience that turned into the best thing in my life."

I rolled my eyes. "You might want to work on your declarations of love."

"I'm telling you the truth. And you know it's the truth, because you feel the same way. When you met me, you did not like me."

"I wouldn't say that."

"Then you'd be lying."

Tex was right. When we first met, it had taken me less

than a second to slot him into the arrogant-entitled-man category. I didn't even know he was a homicide detective at the time, but that fact did little to change my opinion of him. "That's my point. I thought you were an arrogant prig. And how many times have I trusted someone who turned out to be a killer? My judgement of character is wonky."

"Like you said earlier, history shows that sometimes you're right."

"What about this time? I was certain that Jennifer was guilty, so certain that I missed the signs that it was Willow. Willow had access to everything on this ship, and I just accepted her as window dressing." I cocked my head. "How did you know Jennifer wasn't guilty?"

Tex looked uncomfortable. "I didn't."

"Excuse me?"

He shifted again, this time sitting up. He wore a white shirt over his loose navy-blue swim trunks. His deck shoes were neatly tucked under his chair. His mirrored aviator sunglasses kept me from seeing his eyes, but in an uncharacteristic maneuver, he removed them and set them on the deck.

His eyes were crystal blue, bright and clear, bluer than the ocean and the sky and the drinks being handed out by the bar. His hair blew around his forehead in the playful breeze. "I didn't know Jennifer was innocent. A lot of evidence pointed to her being guilty. Everything you said. She was in the water after Homer was stabbed. She had access to him and to the crime scene. Then that bracelet linked her to the thefts. I spent some time with her, and she didn't have great things to say about him. I wasn't ready to lock her up, but I wasn't going to let her out of my sight either. It's why I took her wig. Easier to keep track of a redhead than a blonde."

"You seem to keep track of me just fine."

"That's different."

"If you didn't know she was innocent, then why did you keep telling me it wasn't her?"

"I was trying to keep you safe."

We stared at each other. "Let's make a pact. From this point forward, we tell each other everything."

Tex raised an eyebrow.

"Within reason."

"I don't know if you can handle the truth, Night." He rolled over and folded his hands behind his head. He closed his eyes and basked in the bright sunlight, a playful smile toying with his lips. "But I'm pretty sure your lipstick looked better on me."

CHAPTER THIRTY-THREE

By the time we met Imogene in the parking lot in Galveston, most of my questions had been answered. Rocky was as happy to see me as I was to see him. If I'd bothered to paint on any freckles that morning, they would have been licked off by the time we climbed into the back seat of Imogene's SUV.

Tex and I spent the first hour of the drive telling Imogene about the cruise, the murder, the recovered loot, and the face-off in the Sanctuary. Imogene, a self-proclaimed expert on plotting, pointed out how she would have written the story to tie up more loose ends. She asked more questions than I would have liked about the beach wedding, eventually determining that something shady must have taken place. Neither Tex nor I had anything more to say about that.

I couldn't say much about the rest of the drive home except that the three hours passed quickly after we fell asleep in the back seat.

* * *

"After you complete these outtake forms, I'll cut you a remittance check," Nasty said. She pushed two forms forward, one in front of Tex and one in front of me.

Tex pushed his form back. "No can do. That violates my agreement with the Lakewood Police Department."

"You agreed to this job before we departed," I said. "We were right here in Nasty's office. She needed a married couple, remember? She had a lobby full of couples who answered her ad."

"I can't sign it, but you can," Tex said.

I turned to Nasty. "What happens when I sign this form?"

"You become a freelance partner with temporary employment by Big Bro Security. You'll get a W-9 at the end of the year so you can report the income to the IRS. It's all legit."

"I don't doubt the legitimacy of your business practices, but what does that mean for Tex?"

"If you sign and Tex doesn't, I'll cut the remittance to you. What you two decide to do with your finances is not my business."

I pulled the forms closer. It was a cut-and-dried agreement, outlining the job of investigating a theft on board the *New Nautilus*, the rate Nasty had offered to pay us, and the dates of the trip. I lined out Tex's name and signed mine on the bottom of the form then slid it toward Nasty.

She opened her desk drawer and pulled out a cashier's check. She slipped it into an envelope and held it out to me. It wasn't the first time I'd taken money from Nasty, but it was the first time I wouldn't be expected to pay it back.

Nasty closed the folder. "Overall, what were your thoughts about the cruise?"

"You mean other than the murder, the theft, the hostile

decorator, and the killer pressing a knife into my throat?" I asked.

"Bad investment," Tex said. "Too many internal problems. They're trying to be all things to all people. The *New Nautilus* needs to streamline their concept before they can expand."

"Wait." I held my hand out in front of me. "You're thinking of investing in a cruise?"

"I was," Nasty said, "but not anymore. I told Bogosian it's all his."

"Bogosian…" I looked back and forth between Tex and Nasty's faces. "The cop? What does he have to do with anything?"

Tex answered. "Sam Bogosian is staring down retirement from the Austin PD. He's looking for investments, and he was on the boat to check it out. His position with the police force gave him access to the details of the theft, and he wanted to snoop around and see if their problems were behind them. Scandals can ruin a company, but they can also make them a good deal for new investors before they rebuild."

Everything Tex said was true, and Nasty would have known the exact same thing before the job. I pulled the paperwork toward me again. It was already signed, the payment already transacted, so there was no threat of blowing the whole thing with a bunch of questions.

"Did Texas Luxury Cruises really approach you about managing security on their summer-getaway fleet?"

"No," Nasty said.

"Then this whole thing was a cover to get you access to the boat? Find out if it was a good investment? We weren't sent in to recover stolen merchandise?"

"I read about the thefts in the paper. Once the insurance

company paid out, there wasn't anybody looking for answers. I reached out to them about recovering the stolen property, and they said it had already been written off. Seemed like a good opportunity for some very public press about my company. A way to put Big Bro on a bigger scale."

"You sent us in to see what we could find out about the crime, to see if anybody on the crew was involved. You never expected us to find the loot or catch a killer."

"You do tend to overdeliver," Nasty said.

I tapped the paper and looked at Tex. "We should have asked for more."

He shrugged. "Welcome to public service, Night." He looked at Nasty. "Are we done here?"

"Not quite. You have a decision to make."

"I thought we just did," I said.

"You're a big girl. You can make more than one." She leaned back in her chair. "Before you left for the cruise, I filed for tourist permits on your behalf. Standard procedure."

"And?" Tex prompted.

"There are requirements to being married in Mexico. You two completed four of the five."

"That ceremony wasn't real," I said.

"There was a legitimate justice of the peace. There were questions: do you take this man, do you take this woman. And there were enough witnesses that heard you both say 'I do.'"

"You're not suggesting—"

Tex put his hand on my arm. I shifted my attention to him. "Let's hear her out," he said.

Nasty leaned back. "The only thing you need is a signed marriage certificate. If you want to make it official, I'll pull some strings. If not, you walk away with a story to tell your friends. Your call. I thought you'd want to know."

I sat there, not sure how I felt about that. I shifted my attention to Tex. He stood and held out his hand to me. "You ready to go?"

"Not yet," Nasty said. "I need to talk to Madison alone for a moment."

Tex and I shared a look. I shrugged. "I'll be out front," Tex said.

Nasty waited until the door closed behind Tex then turned her full attention to me. Her hair was back to its regular copper-streaked mane, the braids as distant a memory as the showdown with Willow in my cruise cabin.

"What else could you possibly want? If this is about me and Tex—"

Nasty held up her hand. "It's not what I want. This is about you. There was an employee on the cruise named Persephone. You met her?"

"The decorator?"

"Well, that's the thing. Did you give her some design sketches?"

I nodded.

"She turned them over to the new owners. They were impressed. They'd like to talk to you about a job."

I sat forward. "The new owners want me to decorate the cruise ship. This isn't a hoax?"

"No hoax. I told them the only way I'd bring you their offer was if you had complete transparency."

"Complete transparency," I repeated. I thought over everything that had happened since she first asked me and Tex to take this job. "I think I could live with that."

PILLOW STALK

MADISON NIGHT MYSTERY #1

In case you missed how it all began...

EXCERPT: PILLOW STALK

CHAPTER 1

"Mr. Johnson, I would like to discuss to discuss the disposition of your mother's estate. I understand that you don't live around here—"

"Are you a lawyer?" asked a gruff voice on the other end of a crackly line.

"No, sir, I'm an interior decorator. Madison Night. I own Mad for Mod, on Greenville Avenue--"

"You're a *decorator*? You're calling me about my mom's tchotchkes?"

"I assure you that I mean no disrespect, but in my experience, you are about to be faced with the time consuming challenge of handling your mother's affairs, and I am in a position to take a portion of that challenge off your to-do list." Internally, I cringed at the holier-than-thou tone that had crept into my voice. It was a vocal knee-jerk reaction to people not taking me seriously. "It might interest you that I specialize in mid-century modern design."

"What was your name again? Madison?" he snapped. "What are you, twenty?"

EXCERPT: PILLOW STALK

I was used to people fixating on the least important detail of my phone call, my name. I pushed my long hair away from my face, then used my index finger to free a couple of strands that were stuck by my hairline, thanks to the Dallas-in-May humidity.

"Madison was my grandmother's maiden name," I offered, my head cradled in the kitschy yellow donut phone I used in the office. "I'm forty-seven, and I've been in this industry for over twenty years." The man was obviously more distraught over the death of his mother than the fact that my grandmother's surname had come into fashion sometime in the nineties, but at times like these, minor details could change the course of our conversation.

"My mom didn't have anything valuable. Her whole house was insured for fifteen thousand dollars, and I'd be better off if it had burned down and I got the check. Now I'm stuck with a bunch of junk I could never convince her to throw away."

I wrote *fifteen thousand?* on the side of a real estate flier that sat on my desk and put on my best can-do attitude. "Mr. Johnson, I'm prepared to make an offer on the entire estate. If you accept it, I can bring you a check tomorrow, and you can be on your way back to Cincinnati as soon as tomorrow night."

"Let me get this straight. You're offering to write me a check for stuff you haven't even seen?"

"That's correct."

"Lady, if this is a joke, you have a lousy sense of humor." He hung up on me.

I drummed my fingers against the top of my desk and stared at the flier, temporarily distracted by the overdone graphics and the photo of the woman listing houses. Pamela

Ritter, a recently licensed real estate agent stared up at me, a picture of blonde hair and blue eyes not all that different than my own, though some twenty-years younger. *Blast from the Past!* screamed the heading, above listings for a string of ranch houses on Mockingbird. *Live like a Mad Man!* Promised the copy on the side. Turquoise bubbles filled the background of the paper, and starbursts, outlined in red, gave it a Pow! Bam! Bop! feel.

Pamela had jumped on the new movement to capitalize on all things fifties, thanks to a recent pop culture focus on the Eisenhower era. I'd been nurturing my passion for mid-century decorating since I was a teenager, since I first watched *Pillow Talk* after learning that I shared a birthday with an actress named Doris Day. I surrounded myself with items from the atomic age long before people like Pamela were born, and thanks to my business, I'd found others who shared my interest and appreciated my knowledge. I crumbled up the flier and tossed it at the trash bin. It bounced off the rim and landed on the carpet.

I glanced at the brushed gold starburst clock on the wall and twisted my blonde hair back into a chignon, then secured it with a vintage hairpin. It was ten minutes to six. I could leave early, I reasoned. Nothing was going to happen in ten minutes. I flipped the open sign to closed, locked the doors, and carried the small bag of trash out the back door, hitting the light switch on the way. I emptied the trash into the dumpster and rummaged through my handbag for my keys. That's why I didn't notice the flat tire.

I bent next to the tire and a slash of pain shot through my left knee. After a skiing accident two years ago, after fleeing down a mountain, I was left with a reminder that I had to look out for myself, because no one else would. The chronic pain forced me to acknowledge my limitations. It kept me from doing the kind of things that independent women knew how to do for themselves and Texas women took for granted. And today, it would keep me from getting home to Rock on time.

I went back inside the studio and called Hudson James, my handyman, though the term hardly described our relationship. "What are the chances you're up for rescuing a damsel in distress?" I asked.

"Depends on the damsel."

"I'm at the studio, and I've got a flat tire. I'd try to change it myself," I said, but stopped when the humiliating reality of me calling a man to ask for help resonated in my ears. I never thought I'd be that kind of woman.

"Madison, it's no problem. I'll be there in a couple of minutes."

Hudson's blue pickup truck pulled into the alley by my studio and parked next to the dumpster. His longish black hair had curled with the humidity, the front pushed to the side, behind his ear, the back flipping up against the collar of his t-shirt. "I thought you were calling because you had a job for me," he said.

I flushed. "I might," I said, "I'm still working it out. A woman died—"

He held up a hand. "I don't want to know the details."

"It's just business."

"I look at you and I see sweetness and innocence, not a ruthless business woman."

"Don't let the blonde hair and blue eyes fool you."

"Honey, they had me fooled me the first time I laid eyes on you." He winked and took the keys from my hand. Before he turned back to the car, his eyes swept over my body. "Is that a new dress?"

I looked down at my dress, a light blue fitted sheath dress that was significantly more wrinkled than it had been when I left the house this morning. A series of circles in gingham, stripe, and polka dot had been appliquéd to the neckline and hem.

"It's a new-old dress. Early sixties. From an estate sale in Pennsylvania, before I moved here. The woman died in a car accident—"

"Enough! I like the dress. I like the dress on you. But I don't need to hear the obituary of the woman who owned it first." He disappeared next to the tire.

"It's good for business," I said.

"The dress or the estate sales?"

"The only client I talked to today was over the phone, thank you very much." Maybe things would have gone differently if I had met Steve Johnson face to face. Not because of the dress, but because he'd see that I was legitimate.

Inside the studio, the phone jangled. Technically, Mad for Mod was still open, and even though I'd wanted to leave early, I didn't want to be one of those businesses that skimped on the hours. "Do you mind if I get that?"

"Nah, go ahead. This'll take a couple of minutes."

I picked up the ball of paper by the wastepaper basket and set it on the corner of my one-of-a-kind desk, then reached for the phone. "Mad for Mod, Madison Night speaking," I answered. I heard a click, then a dial tone. I sank into the chair and battled the crumpled up flier back and forth across the slick surface of the desk. It was a gift from Hudson, a hodgepodge of parts from items too damaged to repair. It had cost him more in time and vision than materials, and I wouldn't trade it for anything. More than once I'd asked him to be a partner in my business, and every time he declined. He was reliable, artistic, genuine, and best of all, smelled like wood shavings. In a parallel universe I might have entertained romantic thoughts of him, but life as it was for a single, forty-seven year old business woman with trust issues didn't allow for fantasies like that. And even if I was capable of giving in to attraction, I had long learned one lesson: men may come and go but good handymen last forever.

I closed up the studio for the second time. The phone mocked me from the other side of the back door. I ran back in and answered on the third ring, slightly breathless.

"Ms. Night, this is Steve Johnson. You called me about my mother's estate?" His voice had changed. The gruff had been traded for something else. Maybe the interest in my money. I seized the opportunity for a second chance.

"Mr. Johnson, I know it's unorthodox for me to have made an offer over the phone, but if you have time available tomorrow, I'd be more than happy to meet with you in person."

"That's not necessary. I changed my mind and I'm willing to sell. Call me at this number tomorrow and we'll wrap this thing up."

I grabbed a thick black marker out of the orange Tiki mug on the desk, flattened out Pamela's real estate flier, and scrawled the number across her smiling blonde face. "Perfect," I said, too eagerly, considering the circumstances. And then, for the second time that day, Steve Johnson hung up on me, leaving me to wonder what exactly had happened to change his mind.

ACKNOWLEDGMENTS

Bringing any book to publication is a challenge that starts with a nugget of an idea from me, but in the case of Madison Night, that nugget is always inspired by Doris Day. I am continually inspired by the actress's vast body of work, and in this book, I was able to show aspects of her singing career as well. It is true that she was romantically linked to Sly Stone for a brief moment, but there's no evidence that it was anything other than a rumor.

This book was also informed, in part, by my one and only trip on a cruise. My trip was nothing like Madison's, but it was fun to revisit those memories and remember what stood out to me: lower inflammation in my joints, my rings being loose, and the shrimp cocktail. Highlights!

Thank you to Lynn, Angela, and Irene with Red Adept Editing for your valuable work on this manuscript, and to my local Panera for allowing me to take up a booth three hours a day and write about murder.

Initially, I wanted Rocky to be on the cruise with Madison and Tex, but research indicated there were a lot of considerations I couldn't easily gloss over. Thank goodness for Imogene and the mystery she's been working on since we first met her in book seven!

A special nod to Elizabeth Hollier, Judy Johnson, Sandra Ann Conine Fields, Sydney Cavero-Egusquiza, and Tatiana

Novas for volunteering to be dead people, and to everyone who submitted their names for consideration. You have no idea how much I enjoy your notes in response to this call for participation!

Thank you to the Polyester Posse, for helping to spread the word about this book, and lastly, to my readers. Thank you for spending time with Madison Night and for inspiring me to write another book.

ABOUT THE AUTHOR

Four-time award nominee and national bestselling author Diane Vallere writes smart, funny, and fashionable character-based mysteries. After a career in luxury retailing, she traded fashion accessories for accessories to murder. Diane started her own detective agency at age ten and has maintained a passion for shoes, clues, and clothes ever since.

Get girl talk, book talk, and life talk when you join the Weekly Diva Club at dianevallere.com/weekly-diva.

ALSO BY

Samantha Kidd Mysteries

Designer Dirty Laundry

Buyer, Beware

The Brim Reaper

Some Like It Haute

Grand Theft Retro

Pearls Gone Wild

Cement Stilettos

Panty Raid

Union Jacked

Slay Ride

Tough Luxe

Fahrenheit 501

Stark Raving Mod

Gilt Trip

Ranch Dressing

Madison Night Mad for Mod Mysteries

"Midnight Ice" (prequel novella)

Pillow Stalk

That Touch of Ink

With Vics You Get Eggroll

The Decorator Who Knew Too Much

The Pajama Frame

Lover Come Hack

Apprehend Me No Flowers

Teacher's Threat

The Kill of It All

Love Me or Grieve Me

Please Don't Push Up the Daisies

The Glass Bottom Hoax

Sylvia Stryker Outer Space Mysteries

Murder on a Moon Trek

Scandal on a Moon Trek

Hijacked on a Moon Trek

Framed on a Moon Trek

Warped on a Moon Trek

Material Witness Mysteries

Suede to Rest

Crushed Velvet

Silk Stalkings

Tulle Death Do Us Part

Sheer Window

Costume Shop Mystery Series

A Disguise to Die For

Masking for Trouble

Dressed to Confess

<u>Mermaid Mysteries</u>
Dead in the Water

<u>Non-Fiction</u>
Bonbons for your Brain

Printed in the USA
CPSIA information can be obtained
at www.ICGtesting.com
CBHW031912270824
13785CB00004B/29